THE MAN AT BAY

Richard Savin

1914 is going to be a momentous year …

As murders abound, World War 1 is declared, spymania grips the nation … and Robson, the barman at the Walpole Bay Hotel, invents a new cocktail: the 'Walpole Bay Slammer'.

Copyright Richard Savin

The moral right of the author has been asserted.

Apart from any fair dealing for the purposes of research or private study, or criticism or review, as permitted under the Copyright, Designs and Patents Act 1988, this publication may only be reproduced, stored or transmitted, in any form or by any means, with the prior permission in writing of the publishers, or in the case of reprographic reproduction in accordance with the terms of licences issued by the Copyright Licensing Agency. Enquiries concerning reproduction outside those terms should be sent to the publishers.

This is a work of fiction. Names, characters, businesses, places, events and incidents are either the products of the author's imagination or used in a fictitious manner. Any resemblance to actual persons, living or dead, or actual events is purely coincidental.

© **Richard Savin 2023**

A Grumpy Goat publication
Margate
England

Author's historical note

Throughout the writing of this book I have strived to be as accurate as possible in the description and names of places featured.

However the story is set in 1914, the year of the opening of the Walpole Bay Hotel, and time fogs the record. Places change their names, buildings and streets disappear or are altered to other uses and identities. Resources such as old photographs, newspaper articles and old maps are hugely useful but are also open to the fallibility of interpretation.

One of the major issues I had to contend with was that of coastal erosion, particularly the chalk cliffs. Public record shows that large sections of the chalk were the subject of massive landslip across the years. For example, during the early part of the twentieth century, the whole of the cliff face accommodating the original Captain Digby pub fell into the sea, taking the pub building with it. So the building now existing is not what was there in 1914. What stands on the site today is part of what had been the coach house and stables. This is just one example of the changes time has wrought, and not all of them can be easily uncovered. As a result the topography described in the book is only an interpretation, a construct of my imagination based on what I could find in the record of the day. It is not what the contemporary viewer will see now on a walk along the clifftop.

OTHER BOOKS BY THE AUTHOR

A Right to Bear Arms
http://getbook.at/RBArms

The Girl in the Baker's Van
http://getbook.at/BakersVan

The Boy from the Tangier Souk
mybook.to/BoyTangierSouk

The Girls from New York – Book 1
mybook.to/GirlsfromNewYork

Harley-quin the Grumpy Goat
getbook.at/grumpygoat

The Haunting of the Harlequin Goat
http://getbook.at/harlequingoat

Turn Left at Istanbul
mybook.to/TurnLeft

In the Company of Goats
http://mybook.to/CompanyOfGoats

More Than One Passion
getbook.at/MTOnepassion

Girls and Boys Come Out to Play
mybook.to/GirlsBoysPlay

The Sudden Death of a Cucumber
http://mybook.to/Cucumber

Funny Money … and a girl
https://mybook.to/28Akqt

Candelarbres de Paris
getbook.at/LCP

Hercule Quincompoix
getbook.at/hercule-quincompoix

The Missing Wheels
getbook.at/missingwheels

ACKNOWLEDGEMENTS

My grateful thanks go to all who put their shoulder to the wheel and made this story and its publication possible.

In particular a big thankyou to my editors and proofreaders, Liz and Lin, and especially to Jim for collaboration on the cover design.

A mention also for fellow authors and writers, Ted Yeoman, James and Marie Gault, Cathie Dunn, Linda Amstutz, A L Wall and poet Johanna Lamon for their encouragement, guidance and assistance in the development of the manuscript.

Finally, and certainly not least, I wish to thank the Beta readers: Charlotte Grant, Christina Howes, Sarah O'Neill, and Linda Russell for their invaluable role of appraising the story and giving their critique.

Thank you, everyone.

CONTENTS

- Ch 1 The British Museum Library
- 2 The house in Kensington Church Street
- 3 Margate
- 4 The clifftop
- 5 The American
- 6 The break-in
- 7 Deception
- 8 Useful information
- 9 Red herrings
- 10 Arrest
- 11 More clues
- 12 Contraband
- 13 A trip to London
- 14 Margate again
- 15 Double dealing
- 16 The showdown
- 17 Revelation
- 18 Finale

THE MAN AT THE WALPOLE BAY HOTEL

Chapter 1

The British Museum Library

A small, neatly manicured man made his way through the silence of the Reading Room to where a young woman was sitting at a desk. 'Miss Blain,' he half whispered as he arrived at where the librarian was seated. 'I need a definitive book on British birds. Something with weight and authority. I have to give a talk to the Holborn Ornithological Society. What do we have?'

'I suggest *A History of British Birds*, Mr Meakin; William Yarrell; 1843 edition. It is presently the definitive authority.'

The Man at the Walpole Bay Hotel

'Where do I find that, Miss Blain?'

'Aisle five, under O for Ornithology, Mr Meakin.'

'Thank you.' Meakin hurried away in the direction of aisle five.

A few minutes later he returned with the book. He placed it on the desk in front of Amelia Blain, who removed the ticket from the inside cover, stamped it with the date and handed it back.

'There is a rather strange individual in aisle five, Miss Blain. Have you seen him? He looks foreign.'

Amelia Blain peered over the top of her glasses in the direction of aisle five. 'I can't say I have, Mr Meakin. What do you mean by foreign?'

'Dark eyes, Miss Blain – and a very severe haircut. He is wearing foreign clothes, too.' Meakin threw a glance towards the aisle. 'I would place him somewhere in the Balkans, perhaps. Though he could be German.'

'Oh, are you sure?'

'I think so.'

'Well, I'll keep an eye on him. He could be a book thief, I suppose. There are some rare editions in that section.'

Shortly after Meakin had left, two more unusual men came into the Reading Room. They did not look like people in search of a book; they were poorly dressed, like workmen. They entered the room in a cautious fashion, stood for a moment looking about them, then began to walk slowly along the book aisles. The heads of several readers looked up and turned towards them, disturbed by the presence of the men and the strangeness of their actions. The two men disappeared separately into the depths of different aisles, one going into the first, and the other going further along, to aisle four.

Seconds after they had gone from view, the man from aisle five, who Mr Meakin thought was acting suspiciously, emerged and walked quickly to the door. He pulled it open and left. As the door swung shut behind him, one of the new arrivals stepped out from aisle four. 'Danny,' he shouted and headed for the door, almost running.

The second rough-looking man appeared and he, too, made a hurried exit. He made no attempt to disguise his urgency but simply strode rapidly through the door. Readers dropped their books and heads were lifted in displeasure as the silence was brutally fractured.

In the corridor both men broke into a run, barging past a woman who they pushed aside roughly. 'Hey, watch what you're doing!' she shouted after them.

When they were gone and quiet had again settled in the reading room, Amelia Blain got up from her chair and walked across to aisle five. She was curious to see what that was about – to see what evidence there was of any irregular activity; but there was none. A book or two no longer neatly in line where browsers had pulled them out and not pushed them fully back into their place, but other than that – nothing.

The Man at the Walpole Bay Hotel

It had been a strange interlude in an otherwise ordinary day.

The man who Mr Meakin had judged to be foreign – the man with the dark eyes and severe haircut – walked at a brisk pace in the direction of the Strand. A short distance behind him the two men in rough clothing, who had disturbed the equilibrium of the reading room, followed, staying far enough behind to be discreet.

At Southampton Row the two men stopped. They nodded to a stranger standing by the kerb. The stranger gave a small movement of his hand in acknowledgement, then smartly took up the pursuit. The original two men slowed their place, then melted into the general flow of pedestrians. Their job was done for the moment.

In Kingsway the foreign-looking man boarded an omnibus bound for Victoria and Kensington. The man now following him left it till the last moment, then he too boarded the bus. He went to the open top deck and took a seat. From that vantage point he could see where his quarry alighted without himself being seen.

The omnibus ground its way along the Embankment. When it arrived at Victoria Station he made ready to leave. He stood up and walked to the open staircase at the back, from where he had a clear view of who got off. The bus came to a halt, but his man was not among the passengers who alighted. He went back to his seat.

The Man at the Walpole Bay Hotel

The omnibus turned north, in the direction of Knightsbridge. It stopped at Hyde Park Corner, but the foreign-looking man stayed put. The vehicle groaned along Knightsbridge, its rear axle whining under the load of a full complement of passengers, the gears complaining as they laboured through the traffic.

At Harrods store the quarry still stayed put. Then, as the omnibus stopped at Kensington High Street, the foreign-looking man with the severe haircut finally got off. Just as the vehicle began to continue its journey the follower, too, stepped casually onto the pavement. He took up a position about twenty yards behind his quarry. Together, though separated by anonymity, they set off in the direction of Kensington Church Street.

*

Just before closing time, a woman came into the Reading Room in the Library. Miss Blain was already collecting her things together and preparing to close the doors for the day. 'Hello, Amelia,' the newcomer smiled apologetically. 'I'm so sorry to call on you at the eleventh hour but I need a book. I'm off on an assignment first thing in the morning.'

Miss Blain returned an obliging smile. 'Oh, Lucinda, no need to apologise. I still have one reader left. He's just putting the books he's been reading back in their place. By the way, we had the strangest occurrence earlier. Two very uncouth individuals came in. They acted *so* rudely and caused a bit of a disturbance.'

'I think I saw them,' Lucinda said. 'They pushed past me in the corridor. They were in a roaring hurry. They all but had me off my feet and on the floor.'

'Dear me, how terrible. I have no idea what such rough men were doing here in a library. They did not look like the type to read; more ditch diggers or navvies. Anyway, how can I help? What are you looking for?'

'Oystercatchers. I'm going down to the Kent coast for a week. The museum wants a paper on the oystercatcher numbers along that part of the coast. There are others doing the Sussex bit. I thought I'd come and snaffle the best of the books before anybody else gets to them.'

'Aisle five, Lucinda. Look at the end of the row, under W for Waders. There's some jolly good stuff there.'

Lucinda returned after a short while, two books in hand. 'These should do it. Here's my library card.'

Miss Blain took the card. 'I'll just enter it into the staff register. Lucinda Coates,' she mouthed quietly as she penned the name in a ledger. 'There we go. Which part of the Kent coast are you off to? I hear it is very lovely countryside.'

'Margate; at least that's where I shall be based.'

Amelia Blain looked envious. 'Ooh, I say, that's rather spiffing. I hear it's very fashionable.'

'Yes. I have an aunt living there. I'm rather looking forward to it, actually.'

The Man at the Walpole Bay Hotel

As Lucinda Coates left the reading room, the man who had returned his books to their rightful place emerged from aisle five. 'Thank you, Miss. Sorry to have stayed so late.'

'That all right, err ...,' she looked down at the name on the card he had handed to her, '... Mr Grayson. Have a good evening.'

'Thank you.' He looked at a pocket watch he had fished out of his coat. 'My goodness it is later than I thought. I must hurry or I'll miss my train.'

'Have you far to go?'

'Not really – only as far as Margate.'

Chapter 2

The house in Kensington Church Street

The street was busy, the pavement packed with a homegoing crowd; heads down and tired from the tedium of their day.

Below ground, passengers of the Metropolitan and District Railway sweated as they jostled and struggled up from poorly ventilated platforms to pour out into the still warm July evening air.

Outside High Street Kensington station a paperboy shouted the evening headline. 'Extra, Extra, read all abaht it! Archduke and Duchess shot dead. Extra, extra! Assassination in Serbia.'

A man in a Panama hat, who looked out of place among the dark suits, bowlers and trilbies, proffered a ha'penny. 'I'll take a copy.'

'There yer go, guv.'

The man folded the paper, tucked it under his arm and walked off in the direction of Kensington Palace. A short while later he made his way up Kensington Church Street until he came to a small side street. He stopped on the corner and lingered for a moment. Taking the newspaper from under his arm he made an obvious show of reading it, creating the illusion of a man in no particular hurry. He cast a casual glance up and down the street, then continued walking. At a terrace of town houses he slowed, seemingly looking for an address. He stopped at one and, taking a key from his pocket, opened the front door. Inside the hall was gloomy.

'Ernst,' he called out in a moderate voice. 'Ernst.'

There was no reply. He looked into the first room, just sticking his head inside for a brief moment. He stood in the hall and listened. He called the name again, louder this time. 'Ernst.' Still nothing. He climbed the staircase to the first floor, walked the short length of a landing to a door at the end, opened it and took one step inside. He looked around the room, then stepped back out onto the landing, pausing to listen. The house seemed unnaturally quiet.

Halfway along the landing there were two more doors, one to the left, one to the right. He pushed each one open in turn and looked inside. He was a man in search of something, and he hadn't found it.

He climbed the stairs to the floor above. It was a mirror image of the one below. He opened the first door he came to, glanced inside – nothing. He went to the second door. As he did so he thought he heard a sound. He stopped. 'Ernst. Is that you?'

The Man at the Walpole Bay Hotel

He pushed the door open. Inside, he could smell the iron-scented tincture of fresh blood. He stepped carefully over the body that lay awkwardly sprawled on the floor.
There was a lot of blood.

The victim was a man in his early twenties. The killing must have been very recent, he concluded; the blood was still very red. He didn't bother with a close examination; why would he, it was a corpse. Nothing he could do would help it.

He took a few steps to a heavy triple wardrobe. The drawers were all open but the contents lay relatively undisturbed. It was clear there had been no time for whoever despatched the corpse to make a proper search. He crouched down in front of the wardrobe and pushed an arm underneath. His hand knew exactly where to go and he found what he was seeking: a small notebook, taped to the underside of the massive piece of furniture. He carefully folded it into the newspaper and prepared to leave.

Downstairs, he heard the front door bang shut. His hand went to the inside of his jacket and pulled out a gun. It was a snub-nosed Astra with a long slim silencer screwed into the barrel. He stepped carefully over the corpse and went to the edge of the staircase. There was no sign of anyone. He descended cautiously down to the hall; it was empty. Someone had been there while he was in the house searching. They must have been there when he arrived; hiding when they heard him open the front door. He didn't wait; he wasn't going to hang about.

He slipped the gun back inside his jacket, opened the front door and left, walking briskly until he found a motor cab. 'Take me to the steamer wharf at Hungerford Bridge,' he told the driver. 'Double fare if you get me there in time to catch the last paddler to Margate.'

Chapter 3

Margate

'I saw that man again this morning, Dorothy. Up on the cliffs at Palm Bay. What do you suppose he is doing there? He had binoculars – looking out to sea.'

'Well, I imagine he could be bird watching. There are all manner of wading birds along the estuary, you know.'

'I saw him further along, too; up by the old flint fort. You know, that one on the walk to Kingsgate – it overlooks Botany Bay.'

'Actually, Effie, that isn't a fort. Did you know that? It's just some rich man's folly. It's barely two hundred years old. By the way, my niece is coming for a visit next week.'

'Lucinda, is that the one?'

'Yes. You'll like her. She was up at Oxford; one of the few women. Very bright girl. Works doing research into avian populations for the British Museum.'

'I say, that's rather clever of her. Will she stay long?'

'A week or two as I understand it.'

'That'll be jolly good, Dorothy. Perhaps we shall get all the London gossip. Where is she staying? With you?'

'No, I'm a bit cramped at the moment. Tradesmen, you know; a carpenter and decorators. No, she's staying here. In this lovely new hotel.'

'Oh, that'll be nice for her; she'll like it here at the Walpole Bay. I hear the rooms here are very comfortable.'

'So I'm told, Effie. My friend, Hettie Moncrief, stayed here when she was down. She wrote to me about it. It's right up to the minute, she says. The furnishings in the bedrooms are all the very latest thing. I've not been upstairs to look but I believe it has the most wonderful views from the bedrooms. They say you can see right across the estuary from those on the top floor.'

'Well, that will be nice for Lucinda.'

'Indeed, Effie. She she's very fond of sea views. Ah, there's Simpson,' Dorothy said, changing the subject. She waved to attract the attention of a formally dressed man in a black suit. 'He really is one of the best hotel concierges I have come across.'

The concierge came out onto the veranda where they were sitting. 'We shall need our usual table for lunch – and a little aperitive to sharpen the appetite, I think. Gin and tonic, Effie?'

'Oh rath-er.'

The Man at the Walpole Bay Hotel

*

The train from London arrived late. For the passengers it had been a tedious journey. They had stopped at every village station and signal halt along the route. In Whitstable there had been an unscheduled interruption while the engine took on water.

At Margate, a man in a dark suit alighted. He was carrying a small leather case and wearing a bowler hat. When he emerged from the station he stood for a while and surveyed the view in front of him: a wide arc of pale-yellow sand, flanked at one end by a long harbour wall. In its lee, more than a dozen or so fishing boats sat at anchor. The water was up for the moment, but when the tide went out they would sit there stranded, waiting for the next high water.

On the far side of the harbour arm he could just make out part of a long amusement pier jutting out into deeper water. Spurred off the end there was a landing jetty where he could clearly see a paddle steamer moored: one of the Queen Line steamers, down from London.

On the pavement outside the station there were tables where refreshments were being served. The man sat at one and ordered a pot of tea. He took a newspaper out of his coat pocket, unfolded it and looked again at the headline: GENERAL MOBILISATION AS COUNTRY PREPARES FOR WAR, it trumpeted. His tea arrived; a few minutes later a man in a Panama hat came and sat

The Man at the Walpole Bay Hotel

at his table. 'Grim business,' the newcomer said, tapping a finger on the headline.

'Ah, my dear Mr Donovan.'

The man in the Panama tutted. 'No need to be so formal, Seymour. There's no one to overhear us.'

The man in the bowler smiled. 'I got your message, Harry. What's the problem?'

'Ernst is dead.'

'Is he now. That was careless. How did it come about?'

'Not sure. We were supposed to meet at the British Museum for the exchange – I got held up. When I arrived there the place was closed. I went over to the Kensington house. By the time I arrived they'd already got to him.'

'The Brotherhood?'

'Maybe – or our German friends.'

'Fritz? Well, there's no love lost now. Bound to be a war.'

Harry Donovan cocked his head to one side. 'That'll complicate things. I was hoping for some cooperation from our friends in Berlin.'

His companion picked up his cup and slurped on the tea. 'Not much hope of that. Did they get anything? These villains who despatched poor Ernst.'

'No, I'm sure I disturbed them. I don't think they had time. I've got his notebook. I knew where he kept it.'

'Well, then, that's all right – not for Ernst, of course,' the man called Seymour shrugged. 'Can't be any fun being dead.'

The Man at the Walpole Bay Hotel

'Who can say?' the man in the Panama forced a grin. 'No one ever comes back to tell you. Anyway, I need the body moved. Shouldn't be left there too long; not in this weather – it'll start to smell, then the neighbours'll complain. Next thing you know Scotland Yard will be all over it and through it.'

'That would be awkward; don't want a horde of nosey busybodies causing problems. I'll get the undertakers in. How long have you been here, by the way?'

'I came down the Thames on the steam paddler three days ago.'

The man in the bowler hat pushed his teacup away and stood up. 'Three days? Old Ernst will be getting a bit ripe then. So what about the notebook? Were the papers with it?'

'No, I'm not sure about that. I have to go back to Kensington and do a proper search. His passing shouldn't make too much difference, so long as we find the papers; other than we shall save some cash.'

'How long are you staying, Harry?'

'A week, two weeks. However long it takes.'

'And where are you lodged?'

'The Walpole Bay Hotel. Just up the hill from the town: Cliftonville. It overlooks the bay there. One down from Palm Bay. Got a top floor room. Conveniently tucked away. Handy lookout too.'

'Sounds very nice. Enjoy the view. Oh, and Harry, try not to go the way of Ernst. I can't keep disposing of bodies.'

Chapter 4

The clifftop

A taxi drew up to the kerb in front of the Walpole Bay Hotel. A young woman got out. She was in her early twenties with strikingly red hair and pale green eyes. She paid the driver, refusing his help with her suitcase, and walked up the front steps to the reception. She registered as Miss Lucinda Coates of London, noting her occupation as ornithologist, adding, British Museum. She always did that; she felt it gave her status.

The clerk on the reception desk scrutinised the entry. He looked at the note which had been penned in the column of the register under the heading of 'Special requirements'; two words appeared: 'Sea view'. 'Room 38, miss,' he said politely. 'On the third floor.'

As she headed for the stairs he ran a finger down the book, noting that she was the second guest who had requested a room with a sea view. A

The Man at the Walpole Bay Hotel

point rather lost on him, since all the rooms had views of the sea.

After unpacking her suitcase and checking that the bed was comfortable, Miss Coates went back down the stairs to the lounge. She made her way to where two women in their early middle age were sitting in comfortable armchairs. They were both attired in the latest and most fashionable style with above the ankle floral print dresses, belted at the waist and long fitted velvet jackets. One of them got to her feet. 'Lucinda, it's so nice to see you again, my dear. Are you here for long?'

'At least a week, Aunt Dorothy, perhaps more. I'm to do some research on oystercatchers for the department I work in.'

'Oh, that *is* lovely.' She turned to the woman next to her. 'This is my dear friend, Effie Dalrymple. I've told her all about you, and how clever you are.'

*

The grass on the clifftop was scrubby, choked with weeds and detritus from the dying of past seasons. Across it, with a pair of binoculars slung on his shoulder, Donovan walked quickly, his boots scuffing at the dry chalky earth.

He made his way towards the Botany Bay gap; a steep paved cut through the cliff that led down to the beach. Ernst had been careless to get killed like that, he told himself. He had taken a needless risk going back to the house in Kensington, but worse, he thought, he might have exposed him as well. If that was so, then the whole plan was compromised. There was only one way to find out. He would have to go to the drop-off point. If they turned up, he would know it was still secure.

The tide was out. He could see the chalk arch and the cave beyond. It had not been clear from the notebook if that was in fact the drop point, but the cave *was* the most likely place.

Donovan walked closer to the edge of the clifftop. He could see the whole of the chalk arch now. It stood like an elephant in profile, paddling in the sea; a narrow outcrop that had been detached from the mainland by the erosion of time and the elements. Now it was isolated, twenty yards out from the cliffs. Behind it, where it had once joined the mainland, a cave had been formed – a deep, lofty cavern, carved out by years of harsh winter storms.

It was a place that was naturally camouflaged and not easy to reach. The shore in front of it was littered with chalk boulders from rock falls, and strewn with large, rounded flints. The entrance could be reached only when the tide was fully out. Unless you knew it was there, you would easily pass it by unnoticed.

He cursed as his foot slipped off a large chalk slab, silky with the green slime of wet seaweed. About fifty yards from the mouth of the cave there was another indent in the chalk cliff face, a cleft formed by a recent rock fall. The rubble of the fall had left a convenient mound. From behind it he

The Man at the Walpole Bay Hotel

would be able to keep watch on the cave entrance, unobserved and anonymous.

Satisfied that this *was* the right place, he made his way back up the steep slope. There was a hotel fifty yards from the entrance to the gap. On its front elevation there was a bar in the style of an orangery. It was fully glazed and commanded a view out across the estuary to where the mouth of the Thames emptied into the North Sea. If any vessel approached, it would be visible as soon as it came over the horizon. For the moment he would wait there, he decided. Just before sunset would be time enough to make his move.

The bar was crowded but he found a seat at a window table and, having ordered a pint of bitter, he sat down to wait. Shortly after he had settled in his seat, a man of about his age, in a light suit and straw hat, walked up to his table. 'Do you mind?' he asked politely, and sat down at the table. It was inconvenient; Donovan did not want company, but there was little he could do about it. He tried to avoid eye contact, which might result in conversation but the man leant towards him, obviously intent on talk. 'Ah, binoculars, I see,' he said with enthusiasm. 'Hensoldt, German – good glasses those. Looking at the shipping? Plenty to spot plying through the estuary between here and London.'

Donovan tried to keep it brief, limit the small talk. 'Bird watching, actually.'

'Ah, waders, I suppose. Oystercatchers, is it?'

'Whimbrel.'

'Hah, whimbrel. Probably curlews at this time of year. Very similar bird though they lack quite the same haunting quality in their call. I have heard it said that in the old days, folklore had it their call was the mourning of lost souls. Stranger down here, are we?'

Donovan shuffled uncomfortably. This man was becoming a nuisance. 'Just visiting,' he mumbled. 'A short break – sea air and spot a few birds.'

'Well, the place you should go then is Pegwell Bay,' the man said, grinning with the satisfaction of one who thinks he is being helpful. 'Not far from here. If you set out in the direction of Ramsgate it's just by there …'

Donovan was about to cut him short, make his excuses and leave, but the man pre-empted him. 'Enjoy your stay here. I have to go.' He stood up, swallowed the rest of his beer and made for the way out. Donovan heaved a sigh of relief. The last thing he had wanted was to be noticed.

No sooner had the man with the straw hat left than another unwanted guest came and sat at the table. This was no good, Donovan told himself. He got up and left.

Outside, he went back to the path that ran along the cliff top where he immediately encountered the man in the straw hat. He moved to avoid the man who, on seeing him, waved. Donovan waved back and made off along the path. He walked at a quick pace until he came to what remained of an ancient flint folly in the style of a ruined medieval fort. It was deserted. Inside its walls he could wait and not be seen until he was ready to go down again to the beach.

The light had almost gone when he made his move. He went down the slope to the beach and made for the cleft, where he would be out of sight but from which he could see the mouth of the cave, and the expanse of the shoreline leading to it. He waited for a while. There was nothing but the distant sound of the sea lapping the shore. After what seemed an eternity he heard it: the muted thud, thud, thud of a donkey engine. Then the outline of a small boat. It beached and when it did, he saw them; he wasn't sure how many. Dim smudgy figures in the dusk, perhaps a dozen of them. They came in pairs across the sandy foreshore, then stumbled their way through the boulders and rubble towards the cave. As they got closer, he could see them more clearly. Each man was bent forward under the weight of the boxes they were carrying; long narrow boxes, the size of a child's coffin. Two men to a box, one on each side, hanging onto the rope handles. They worked silently in relays, without a word detectable. Four times they made the trek up from the water's edge, where they had beached their motor pinnace. He knew they could not have come far in a boat of that size. There had to be a larger ship out there somewhere.

He waited until the last box had been landed, and he heard the familiar thud as the donkey engine was cranked into life, before he moved. The tide was coming up; there would be no time to

The Man at the Walpole Bay Hotel

pry into what was in the boxes. That would have to wait for the next low water, though he was certain in his mind that it was the expected consignment. As they sank into the darkness, Donovan retreated back up the narrow slope to the vantage point above.

From the cliff top he scanned the horizon. He could just make out the diminishing pinnace, but little else. Even with the binoculars, there was insufficient light. There was nothing more he could do.

'Hello, again.' A voice behind him made him jerk round defensively. It was the man from the hotel, the birdwatcher who'd spoken to him earlier.

'You won't see curlews along here, old chap; only oystercatchers and turnstones. And not at this time of night.'

'No,' Donovan said. He ran his eyes suspiciously over the man. Was he dangerous? Had he seen anything? He could take no chances.

Donovan made his way back along the cliffs in the direction of Margate. Walking with an urgent stride, from time to time looking back over his shoulder; unsure of whether he might be followed.

Fifteen minutes later, two bays along, he saw the welcoming lights of the Walpole Bay Hotel.

'Good evening, sir,' the receptionist called to him as he stepped into the lobby. Donovan raised a hand in acknowledgement and carried on straight through to the lounge bar.

The Man at the Walpole Bay Hotel

In one corner of the lounge, Dorothy, her niece Lucinda and her friend Effie Dalrymple, were enjoying an after dinner digestive, seated in plush armchairs. Dorothy leant across to her niece. 'There's that man I was telling you about, Lucinda. The one Effie and I keep seeing on the beach. He seems rather solitary really. He's always out on his own.'

Lucinda looked across the room to where Donovan was leaning on the bar.

Effie winked at her friend. 'He is rather handsome, don't you think, Dorothy?'

'He is, Effie. What do you think Lucinda, dear?'

Lucinda seemed unimpressed. 'He's all right in a suave sort of way, I suppose. Not really my type, though. Actually, he's staying in the room next to mine. Always very polite when I pass him in the corridor. I suppose I should try to be more neighbourly to him.'

*

'Good morning, Miss Coates,' the woman at the desk called to her as she stepped off the last tread of the stairs and entered the main reception. 'Will you be taking breakfast?'

'Yes, thank you.'

The receptionist pointed to a pair of glass-panelled doors. 'Through the lounge bar, miss, then straight ahead is the dining room.'

A waiter led her to a table and pulled out a chair; when she was seated he handed her a menu card.

'I can recommend the traditional English breakfast, miss.'

Lucinda Coates shook her head. 'Just the cornflakes thank you – then I shall take some toast; with marmalade, please. You do have marmalade?'

'Of course, miss.'

On one side of her place setting was a neatly folded copy of the local newspaper. The headline bannered: GERMANY MOBILISES. IT IS WAR.

Following the assassination of Archduke Franz Ferdinand and his consort, the Duchess Sophie, Germany and Austria-Hungary are preparing for war with full mobilisation, Prime Minister Asquith has said today. In an address to the Elysée Palace, President Raymond Poincare stated, 'France is ready and will respond with its own mobilisation ...

'Well,' she said to the waiter when he returned with a bowl of cornflakes, 'if that doesn't take the cake. A bit close to here, wouldn't you say?'

The waiter raised an eyebrow. 'A dark lot those Germans, if you ask me, miss. Especially that Mr Bismarck.'

'No, no, not that,' Lucinda picked up the paper and pointed. 'I mean this.'

Tucked away on a side column there was another heading. 'Here, read it for yourself,' she insisted.

It was headed, 'Death at Botany Bay. Body Found on Beach.'

The waiter took out a pair of pince-nez, settled them onto his nose and read the piece.

The body of a man in his early thirties was found at the foot of the cliffs on the beach of Botany Bay early this morning by a dog walker. Mr Harold Harkness, who was out early with his dog Sapphire when they made the discovery, told this reporter there was blood on the rocks where the body lay and he thought the man had slipped on some seaweed, or tripped and cracked his head. Local police say they are unable to comment on the cause of the death at this moment. The body is believed to be that of a local man, Mr Benedict Grayson. Detective Inspector (Artful) Archie Page, who is leading the investigation into the event, said, 'it is too early to make any comment on the circumstances surrounding the death.' However when asked, he refused to rule out foul play.

Mr Grayson was wearing a light-coloured suit at the time and is known to have been drinking at the Fayreness Hotel prior to the incident. The Inspector has appealed for anyone who may have information to come forward and call at the Margate Police Station next to the town hall, where they will be treated with all due confidentiality.

The waiter finished reading and laid the paper on the table. 'Well, that is a bit shocking.'

'That's just along the cliffs, isn't it? Botany Bay?'

'Indeed, miss, not much more than a mile from us, just the other side of Palm Bay. Very close to home.'

'Poor man, what a dreadful thing to happen. Do you suppose it was foul play?'

The waiter shook his head, a grave but doubting expression on his face. 'I can't say, miss, though I do know of the gentleman. He sometimes came here for his afternoon tea. He was a quiet, unassuming man who kept himself to himself, so to speak. He lived alone and liked his hobbies. He was something of an amateur bird watcher, and he had a keen interest in boats as well. There is a little bit of a story attached to him, miss. I understand he was a merchant seaman but gave it up when he suddenly came into money. Probably an inheritance, though there was a rumour it might have come from another source. Shall I bring you your toast, miss?'

'Yes, please do. I suppose we shall have to wait for what the police have to say.'

'Well, if Artful Archie's on the case you can be sure it will be soon. A regular bloodhound that policeman.'

The Man at the Walpole Bay Hotel

After breakfast she set out with field glasses and a notebook. From the hotel to the beach was less than a hundred yards. Although the area was noted for its flocks of oystercatchers she decided she would go further afield; the day was fine and she could combine her task with a bit of a promenade. She walked east along the clifftop until she came to the next bay, Palm Bay. There she encountered a small pavilion. It was an elegant open-fronted construction; a roof supported by slender iron columns with brightly painted timber cladding enclosing the other three sides. The benches under its canopy afforded an enchanting view of the estuary and the North Sea beyond, and for a moment she was tempted to loiter and just sit for a while.

'It's that man again.' She almost said it out loud. He was ambling along, his binoculars case swinging on a strap from his shoulder, a Panama hat on his head, the brim pulled down to shade his eyes from the morning sun. There was another man with him, a man more soberly dressed and wearing a bowler hat; clearly the more suitable for London than a seaside walk. He looked oddly out of place there on the clifftop promenade; too formal for the season, and the location.

They passed within a few yards of where she was sitting, and when they saw her she felt the need to acknowledge them. She waved and shouted, 'Good morning, beautiful day.'

The man in the Panama waved back, but his companion just shot her a rapid glance, then looked away.

The Man at the Walpole Bay Hotel

She watched them go, heading in the direction of the next bay along, Botany Bay, then she made her way down one of the steep gaps that led to the foreshore. The tide was ebbing low and the beach was walkable for as far as she could see. It was not long before she was rewarded with what she came for: a knot of oystercatchers strutting the water's edge, beaks down in the weed, stabbing at mussel shells and ferreting out small crabs. Near them a flock of sandpipers were skittering back and forth on busy spindly legs.

Half an hour of observations and note taking brought her to a point along the foreshore where she could see a chalk outcrop with what looked like an archway eroded through its centre. She lifted her field glasses to get a better look. 'Well, I'll be jiggered,' she said out loud. It was that man again; the one at the Walpole Bay Hotel. At that distance she could not make out the features of his face, but she could clearly see his Panama. Then his companion, the man in the bowler hat, appeared as if from nowhere. She continued to walk in their direction and thought she might engage them in conversation, but then the beach tucked into a curve in the cliff, shielding them from her view. When she came out of it they were gone.

*

'It's been a most curious day, Aunt Dorothy.'
'Has it? How so, my dear?'

The Man at the Walpole Bay Hotel

'Well, I saw our man again, down on the beach this morning. You know, the chap with the Panama who's staying in the room next to mine.'

'Ah, the bird watcher.'

'Well, is he? His companion didn't look at all like he might be. They were along the beach from here, at Botany Bay. There's rather an interesting cave there; huge. They seemed to be stooging around in it.'

'Ooh, that does seem a bit odd. Ah, look, here's Effie. Just in time for tea.' Dorothy looked at her watch. 'Or how about a cocktail, or would that be a bit naughty at this hour. Effie,' she called out, 'come and sit down.'

'Lucinda, my dear,' Effie said effusively, 'so nice to meet you again. Would you be an angel and see if you can find a waiter? I rather fancy a gin and Italian. How about you, Dorothy?'

Chapter 5

The American

Dorothy and, Effie Dalrymple lingered for a while near the harbourmaster's office, just at the point where the harbour arm joined with the main road. The day was busy with promenaders: tourists and residents mingling together, all intent on taking in the bright morning air, and the far-reaching views. The two women went to the railings and looked out across the long golden sweep of Margate Sands.

'How clear it is,' Dorothy remarked. 'You can see the Towers right along the coast quite distinctly.'

'Yes,' her friend agreed. 'I do so like that view.'

A little further into the town a Gothic clock tower rose up from a traffic island in the middle of the road. It chimed a musical introduction then sombrely struck the hour. 'Eleven o'clock,' Dorothy remarked casually. 'It's such a fine morning, Effie. Why don't we walk along – as far

The Man at the Walpole Bay Hotel

as the pier. We can watch the London-bound paddler depart.'

'Oh yes, that would be nice.'

On the jetty at the end of the pier, the paddle steamer *Margate Queen* was preparing to cast off; the last of the passengers were boarding. A long blast from the steam whistle alerted would-be passengers that departure was imminent. An officer with a tin megaphone leaned over the side rail, scanning the pier for the final travellers. He put the horn to his mouth. 'All aboard, all aboard! Five minutes to cast-off.'

At the foot of the boarding stairs a man in a three-piece corduroy suit, wearing a cloth cap, paused, one hand on the rail as if making ready to climb aboard. He was big and heavily set with a bushy moustache.

Next to him another man, smaller and wearing a stained and battered trilby, was deep in conversation. The bigger man seemed to be taking his leave but at the same moment having some kind of an argument. His voice was raised and his accent clearly American.

'It was the wrong man, Jacko. You got the wrong one,' the smaller man in the trilby said irritably.

The bigger man shrugged. 'How the hell was I supposed to know? It looked like the right one to me. See here, pal, you said to look out for a guy wearing a Panama, carrying field glasses, and drinking in that hotel.'

The Man at the Walpole Bay Hotel

'That's sure I did,' the man in the trilby asserted in an accent that clearly marked him out as Irish.

'So this guy checks out on all three accounts. He seemed like the right one to me.'

'Well, he wasn't; so you'll have to find the right man – and make the proper arrangements this time.'

'Uh, uh, I can't hang around here any longer. My job was to see the cargo landed. That is all, full stop. Deals on the side were not part of the agreement. Count that as a bonus if you want.'

'A man is dead. Now you have to go out there and put things right.'

At the same moment of that conversation, Effie and Dorothy arrived to admire the paddler. Hearing some of the remarks, they both looked at each other, mildly shocked by what they had heard. Neither of the men engrossed in the conversation seemed even marginally aware of the two women. The conversation started to become heated. Dorothy pulled on her friend's arm and they both moved several yards away, not wishing to hear more. Oblivious, the two men continued their conversation.

'Too bad, these things happen. I have to ship back to Boston. Anyway, how can you be sure he was Kosher? He looked suspicious as hell to me. He had binoculars, he was looking out to sea.'

'The word I'm hearing is he was a bird watcher. People are suspicious.'

'An accident. He got too close to the edge. It was dark, he tripped and fell off the cliff. Simple. An accident.'

The Man at the Walpole Bay Hotel

'The police will be suspicious, for sure.'

'The cops are always suspicious. That's what they get paid for. It's in their nature, it's how they are. That's why they become cops and not bank clerks, or some other damn thing.'

The man in the trilby looked agitated. 'That still doesn't solve my problem.'

His companion thought for a moment. He shrugged; a quick twitch of the shoulders. 'I didn't come to solve your problems – just to get the damn cargo landed.' He thought some more. 'Tell you what. When I get to London I'll send a cable. There's this guy in New York. Meantime, I suggest you speak with your own people. There must be someone who could do the work.'

With that he held out a hand to shake, then strode up the steps to the deck. Minutes later, with three more blasts on the whistle, the paddles churned and the *Margate Queen* moved off her mooring. The man in the trilby watched for a while then turned. Making his way back along the pier he crossed the promenade and disappeared into the town.

'How extraordinary,' Dorothy remarked, sounding a little shocked. 'Do you suppose we heard that right?'

Effie shook her head. 'I'm not sure I really understood what was being said. They *were* foreigners, so it could be anything.'

'Yes,' Dorothy said, dismissing it lightly; then her voiced almost laughed. 'Perhaps they were anarchists.'

'Oh my goodness. Not in Margate surely.'

The Man at the Walpole Bay Hotel

*

Three hours after leaving its berth, the *Margate Queen* arrived at the mouth of the Swale, where it came alongside the town quay at Queenborough to pick up passengers and take on small cargo. The American in the corduroy three-piece suit ambled down the boarding gangway and stepped onto the dock. It was an unscheduled leaving, but he was a cautious man, mindful that there were those who would happily see him dead.

He stood for a while on the quay, watching the porters carrying boxes and cases on and off the vessel. He made a pretence of interest in the operations of the shoreside crane, as it winched a net of mixed cargo onto the deck of the *Queen*. All the time his eyes furtively flicked from side to side, taking note of the scene and the people around him. He could not afford to be careless; there was suspicion everywhere.

'Right, Jacko, me boy,' he said under his breath, 'I think we should be off.' He set out walking briskly and made his way to the railway station. There he took the branch line to Sheerness, where he boarded the train for St Pancras, London.

Sitting comfortably in a second-class carriage he submerged into the anonymity of his surroundings, satisfied that he had covered his tracks.

At St Pancras the newspaper boys were shouting. 'Germany invades Belgium, read all abaht it! Git yer paypah!'

The Man at the Walpole Bay Hotel

Jacko fished a penny out of his pocket and dropped it into the open palm of one of the boys. The lad pulled a folded copy of the *Daily Express* from under his arm and slapped it into Jacko's hand, 'There ya go, guv.' Jacko tucked the paper into his side pocket and headed for the street. Behind him the boy took up the cry of his wares again. 'Paypah, paypah, git yer paypah!'

Out on the pavement, he stopped briefly to light a cigarette, using the moment to check that he did not have company. Convinced he was not being followed, he walked the short distance to Euston Station and climbed the steps to the concourse. Inside the main hall he bought a ticket for the underground to Waterloo.

As the carriages creaked and rattled through the dark tunnel of the Northern Line he unfolded the newspaper and read the headline. Under the banner it said the Liberals, who had opposed war, were so enraged by what they called the '*rape of Belgium*' that they had now joined with the Conservatives and had voted to serve the German ambassador with an ultimatum to withdraw, on pain of a declaration of war.

In a separate column it trumpeted, '*Spies At Large: 21 arrested. Public warned to be vigilant.*'

A faint smile hovered at the corners of Jacko's mouth. 'That'll keep them occupied,' he thought in quiet satisfaction.

At a shop with a sign saying 'TELEPHONE FROM HERE' he stopped and went in. He lifted the receiver and pressed it to his ear. A moment later the voice of an operator asked what number

The Man at the Walpole Bay Hotel

he wished. He was invited to put some money into the coin box, then he waited.

'I'm hanging loose at the Metropolitan Hotel. Call me when you know what you want me to do. They want me to go back to Margate; finish the job. That's okay – but I need to know. Make it quick. I have my return passage Stateside, booked. With this goddamned war starting, I don't wanna hang around here too long.' He hung up, then went to the shop counter. 'I need a pack of cigarettes. Do you stock Camel by any chance?'

The shopkeeper motioned to a place across the road. 'Try there; they carry all kinds of foreign imports.'

'Thanks, bub,' Jacko said, and left.

*

The man who, some hours before, had been on the Margate jetty talking to Jacko, walked as far as the centre of the town. At the Wellington Hotel he stopped and, after briefly glancing around him, he pushed on the door of the public bar and went in. The light in the room was dim, hazed with the rich smoke of cheroots and coarse pipe tobacco; all mingled with the low hum of conversation rising from the knots of men lounging at rough wooden tables.

'A pint of the black stuff,' he told the barman. 'Is Daniel here?' he asked after the man had pulled a pint of stout and put it down in front of him.

The barman nodded in the direction of one of the tables. 'Over there, Tommy.'

The Man at the Walpole Bay Hotel

With the trilby in one hand and the pint in the other, Tommy went over to one corner of the bar and sat down. 'Danny boy,' he said to the man already seated there.

'Tommy. How's the world?'

'Not good, Danny boy, not good. Our American friend, he's gone back.'

'A problem with the cargo, is it then?'

'No, no, the cargo's fine and all, Danny. It's just our friend left unfinished business.'

'And what would that be then?'

'T'was the wrong man he got to meet.'

'I see, I see. So, the wrong man, was it?'

'It was.'

'And the paper? Do we have it?'

Tommy shook his head. 'Still out there. I think yer man might have it; in which case we have to deal with him. You might be talking with the boys back home. We need a resolution – or it'll be the worse. I'll leave it with you then, Danny, shall I?'

*

Lucinda Coates took a last look in the mirror before leaving her room. She pushed at her hair that was curled tightly over her ears, pleased with what she saw. The swept-up fussy style with everything piled up on the top of the head was going out of fashion. That had been fine for her aunt's generation, but the young wanted something more modern; easier to manage and in keeping with the changing times. As she closed and locked the door, the occupier of the next room stepped out and set off along the landing to the stairs. It was definitely the same man she had seen on the clifftop, she noted. She recognised him from the Panama he was wearing. As he got to the stairway he stood to one side and waited for her to pass him. He raised the Panama in courtesy. 'Good morning, miss,' he said, offering her a smile, which she graciously returned with a small nod of her head.

In the lobby she stopped by the reception to enquire if they had a map of the area and a plan of the town. From there she headed for the restaurant, making her way to the same table she had used since she had arrived. It was neatly set in a box bay window, close to the veranda with a fine view out to the sea. However, when she got there she was surprised to see the man with the Panama hat occupying what she considered to be her place. 'Excuse me,' she said firmly, 'but I think this is my table.'

The man quickly stood up. 'I do beg your pardon, miss,' he said, stepping away and pulling out the chair for her. He looked around for an alternative, but the restaurant was already filled with those wishing to take breakfast. He held out a hand to attract a passing waiter.

'Can you find me a table?' The waiter stood for a moment, looking around him.

'I am afraid it is fully occupied for the moment, sir.' He looked at his watch. 'If you would care to come back in an hour?'

'Ah,' the man shrugged. 'Is there anywhere else locally? Somewhere I might get my breakfast?'

The Man at the Walpole Bay Hotel

The waiter shook his head. 'There is Smith's Hotel along the Esplanade. It's a bit of a walk I'm afraid, sir. That is the nearest.'

'Why don't you sit here,' Lucinda offered, pointing to the vacant chair opposite her. 'It would seem rather churlish of me to deprive you of your breakfast.'

'That's most gracious of you, miss. Thank you.' He drew out the chair and sat down. 'Henry Donovan. But please, call me Harry. Everyone does.'

'A pleasure to be of service, Harry. Lucinda Coates. So what brings you to the wonderful resort of Margate? A holiday perhaps?'

Henry Donovan smiled. 'Relaxation, Lucinda. A break from the stale airs of London, a chance to roam in the open countryside – and see if I can spot some of our feathered friends.'

'You are a bird watcher, Harry? How interesting; ornithology is part of what I do in my work. I'm at the British Museum.'

'Ah.' Donovan seemed slightly wrong-footed by her remark. 'I'm only an amateur though,' he said quickly, 'strictly for the leisure.' He picked up the newspaper that had been left at each table. 'War,' he said, pointing to the headline. 'Looks like there is going to be a war with Germany.'

Lucinda nodded. 'So it would seem. Tell me, if it is not too impertinent of me to ask. What is your occupation?'

'Occupation. Yes, well, I suppose you could say I'm rather between occupations at the moment.'

'And when you are not between, what then?'

The Man at the Walpole Bay Hotel

Donovan pulled a screwed-up sort of face. 'Hmm, difficult to describe; sort of sociologist, I suppose. Not very interesting.'

'Oh, I should have thought that was fascinating.'

'No, no. Tell me about you. I am sure that will be much more interesting.'

At that moment the waiter came to their table. 'There is a telephone call for you, sir – at reception. May I take your order for breakfast, miss?'

Donovan had still not returned by the time she had finished her breakfast. She was reading the newspaper when the waiter came to clear her table. 'What happened to the gentleman who joined me?' she asked him.

'He was called away urgently on some errand or other – as far as I understand it, miss.'

'How curious,' she said. 'What kind of errand? Did he say?'

The waiter looked blank. 'I have no idea. Though I believe it was to do with his work.'

'Work? Are you sure? Now that is strange.'

*

Donovan walked rapidly in the direction of the town. After five minutes he passed Smith's Hotel. After another ten minutes he arrived at Dalby Square. In the square he found what he was looking for: The Dalby Rooms Guest House. He climbed the steps and pushed on the front door. Inside, a woman was sitting on a high stool behind

The Man at the Walpole Bay Hotel

a tall counter. She looked up from the paper she was reading. 'Good morning. How may I help you, sir?'

'I am looking for one of your guests; a Mr Seymour Trevelyan.'

The woman pointed to a door marked Dining Room. 'In there, sir. He is taking his breakfast.'

There were a handful of guests seated at the tables. Donovan crossed the room to one and drew out a chair. Trevelyan said nothing, he simply raised his eyebrows.

'Seymour, we have another problem.'

'We have a lot of problems, Harry. To which one in particular do you refer?'

'It's that girl, the one we passed; up there by the bandstand the other day. She's staying in my hotel.'

'And?'

'She asked what I was doing here. I told her I was a bird watcher.'

'Sounds reasonable.'

'It turns out she is a professional ornithologist; I know bugger all about birds – except they flap their wings and fly.'

'Hmm, I see how that might be awkward. Perhaps you should buy a book and bone up on our feathered friends.'

'I expect better than that, Seymour. I'm suspicious of her. What's she doing here anyway?'

'Birdwatching, by all accounts.'

'There's something else too.'

Trevelyan took a sip of tea. 'And that is?'

'I've been going through Ernst's notebook. I might have found something regarding the missing document. It's the last entry he made. It must have been shortly before he was killed.'

'What does it say?'

'It's not very precise but it looks like Ernst did leave the documents hidden in a book – in the ornithology section.'

Trevelyan screwed up his mouth and raised his eyebrows. 'So the girl – what did you say her name was?'

'Lucinda.'

'So you think she might have the papers?'

'Not sure. I'm working on it. It's clear Ernst hid it somewhere in that section of the library.'

'Hmm, why would he do that?'

'I don't know. Maybe he was followed. Maybe he didn't trust us to play fair with the deal. It could be that he hid it somewhere till he'd got his hands on the money. That's what I'd do. Hide it and then after I'd counted the cash, pass on the location.'

'Well, you would because you, Harry, are a person who places little faith in your fellow man.'

'Cautious, Seymour; just being careful. These are difficult times. Lives could be lost.'

Trevelyan put on an urbane smile. 'Too many already I fear, Harry.'

'What about that chap sent flying off the clifftop? What do we know about the investigation?'

'Not a clue, dear boy. Now that our flat-footed friend, the good Inspector Page, is investigating I

The Man at the Walpole Bay Hotel

advise that we steer clear of the matter. The event shouldn't concern us further.'

Trevelyan drained his teacup and put it down precisely on the saucer. 'We have to find the papers, Harry. Without them our hands are empty. The papers tie the consignment they landed to the supplier. Get it or we have nothing.'

'Where is the consignment now?'

'On its way to Bristol, I imagine. We have about a week, Harry. After that we shall have missed the boat – literally. We have to find those papers. We don't have much time. Work on the girl. See if she has them.'

Chapter 6

The break-in

Lucinda Coates congratulated herself on a productive morning. Immediately after breakfast she had gone to the area of Westbrook, on the road out of the town. She had been told of a colony of oystercatchers that regularly fed at Nayland Rock, a local chalky outcrop which was uncovered when the tide was out.

The location proved most convenient as there was a large hotel by the shore; she was able to take lunch in its conservatory restaurant, and continue her observation of the birds.

By two o'clock the tide had risen, covering the rocks, and the birds had gone. That was it for the day, she decided, and thought she might give some time to exploring the town.

When she got back to her room at the Walpole Bay, she saw the door was ajar and there was someone inside. One of the room maids, she

The Man at the Walpole Bay Hotel

automatically supposed; come to clean and make up her bed. She pushed on the door, then stopped abruptly. It was not what she was expecting and, for an instant, she stood rigidly still. It wasn't the room maid – it was him; the man from the room next door, the man who had sat at her table over breakfast – Harry Donovan.

The room was a mess. All the drawers in the dressing table had been pulled out and the contents dumped on the floor. The wardrobe gaped wide open, the clothes and hangers dropped carelessly, all jumbled together where they had fallen. The bedclothes had been pulled off and the mattress showed signs that it had been lifted. Even the rugs had been turned back, pushed aside.

Lucinda stared in horror at the sight of her silk cami-knickers strewn around, exposed for anyone to see – and, worst of all, there *he* was, standing in the middle of it all. She shuddered. It was as if she had been violated.

'*What do you think you are doing!*' The words came out half strangled, half shouted. She instinctively clutched a hand to her throat. '*Get out of my room! How dare you!*' Her response had been instinctive, outraged. It was quickly followed by a sense of threat. He put up a hand. Lucinda flinched, thinking he was about to strike her.

'No, no, wait a minute. It's not what it seems,' he said quickly defensive. 'I heard a sound. I was in my room. A sort of bang, like someone falling. I came to investigate – I found it like this. I think you have been burgled.'

The Man at the Walpole Bay Hotel

She stood in abject silence for several seconds, absorbing the shock of what lay around her. 'Excuse me,' she said in an irrational reflex of politeness, and pushed past him. She began to gather up the exposed lingerie.

'I think you should leave everything as it is,' he told her quietly. 'Ask the reception to call the police. They will not want anything touched until they have had a chance to investigate. Would you like me to tell them?'

She nodded, still in an abstract state of limbo. 'Yes please, if you would.'

*

In Margate town police station, Detective Inspector Archie Page was reviewing what little evidence there was concerning the death of Benedict Grayson, whose body had been found by the base of the cliff at Botany Bay. Short of the body there was little to go on.

'Well,' he said to the station sergeant, 'what have we got? A man falls off a cliff in the dark of the night. Accident? Suicide? Or perhaps we are looking at a little skulduggery. What do you think Sergeant? Did he fall, did he jump – or was he pushed?'

The sergeant screwed up his mouth and wagged his head questioningly, but offered no suggestion.

'Was he local, Sergeant?'

'Yes, sir. Mr Grayson lived close by. Just up the road. Known to the staff and regulars at the hotel.'

'I see. So he'd know the lie of the land?'

The Man at the Walpole Bay Hotel

'I would have thought so, sir.'

'Hmm. So, unlikely he would have strayed too close to the edge and fallen?'

'Does seem improbable, sir.'

'Suicides usually leave a note. Goodbye to the rotten world. That kind of thing.'

'Of course, sir. That is the normal way.'

'There was no note?'

'Nothing's been found, sir.

'So – that leaves us with skulduggery, Sergeant.'

'I would think so, sir.'

'Well, where there's foul play there's usually clues. Is my driver around?'

'In the tea rooms across the way, sir.'

'Good, fetch him please. I think another visit to the scene is next; and while you're about it find me a plain clothes detective constable to come with me and take notes.'

*

The black angular shape of a Crossley motorcar lumbered up to the Fayreness Hotel and scrunched to a halt on the gravel. DI Page opened the door and stepped out. From the back seat a fresh-faced detective constable emerged. Page stood for a moment, surveying the grass area that lay between them and the cliff edge. 'Right lad, let's take a look.'

The grass they walked across had been mown short, but as they came to the cliff there was a strip that had been left uncut just where it ran close to the edge. Page went to the margin of the uncut

The Man at the Walpole Bay Hotel

grass. He pointed to where it had been trodden down.

'Interesting; signs of activity.' He crouched down to examine an area that had been crushed. The ground was dry and dusty. 'Make a note lad: heel print in the loose dust – and a very nice one, too.'

The DC scribbled in a notebook. 'What's that, sir?' He moved a few paces further along and bent down to inspect something. 'Field glasses, sir.'

Page stood up. 'Now that *is* interesting. Pick them up by the strap, lad. Keep your paws off them, though, they'll need dusting for prints.'

Page looked at the dangling glasses. 'Right, let's go and have a talk with the hotel staff – see if anyone can shed some light. And use their phone to call the station. We need someone up here to make a cast of the heel print before it gets rubbed out.'

In the Fayreness Hotel, the manager found a waiter who had been present at the time Grayson and Donovan had briefly met.

DI Page stood the field glasses on the bar counter. 'I believe you knew the deceased, Benedict Grayson. Is that correct, son?'

'Yes, Inspector. He was a regular. Very nice man he was too. Always polite – and a good tipper at Christmas.'

'You were here serving, I understand – on the night of the incident? Is that correct?'

'I was, sir.'

'Did you see anyone with him, by any chance?'

The Man at the Walpole Bay Hotel

The waiter nodded his head in slow deliberation. 'He came in alone; he usually did. There *was* someone I saw him talking with. I know because I was clearing up glasses from the next table, and I was going to take the one from the gent he was talking to, but he hadn't drunk it all.'

'What was he like – this gent? Can you remember anything about him?'

'Tall; you could tell that even when he was sitting. Well dressed. Quite ordinary really.'

'What about his face? Anything special? Beard, perhaps, moustache, maybe?'

'I seem to remember he had a beard, sir. A bit like our King George.'

'Hair colour?'

'Ordinary, sir, sort of darkish.'

'Anything else?'

The waiter thought for a moment. 'Not really. Oh, and he had a Panama hat. I noticed that because it had a very unusual silver and blue band round it. They're normally black.' The DC made a note.

'What about these?' DI Page pointed to the field glasses. 'Recognise these, do we?'

The waiter went to pick them up but Page put out a hand to stop him. 'No, don't touch. Just take a close look.'

'I think those belonged to Mr Grayson, sir. He usually carried binoculars. He was a keen birdwatcher – and he was interested in ships. We get a lot of ships mooring just offshore; waiting to go up to the London docks they are, sir.'

The Man at the Walpole Bay Hotel

'Right,' Page turned to the DC, 'off you go and phone the station. I'm going to stand guard by that shoe print before some clod tramps all over it.'

A uniformed constable on a bike came pedalling furiously across the grass to where Page had mounted guard. 'Message from the Sarge, sir. There's been a burglary. Someone's turned over a guest's room in the Walpole Bay Hotel. He thought you ought to know, sir.'

Page gave a disinterested shrug. 'Right ho, Constable. I'll call in there on my way back.'

'Good. That looks like the forensics, Constable,' DI Page pointed to where a black Ford van had pulled up in front of the hotel. 'Over here,' he shouted and waved an arm in the air. The forensics men saw him and set out in his direction.

'That's what we need casting,' Page said, when they arrived, indicating the impression in the dust. 'Can we manage that – it's none too stable?'

One of the men gave the imprint a cursory inspection. 'Should be all right, Inspector. Lucky really; looks like it might rain later. Probably got it in the nick of time. We'll take a photograph first, though – just in case the cast doesn't work.'

Page stood back to watch; a sense of satisfaction that they had such a useful clue. 'Shouldn't be hard to match. When they're done, Constable, I want you to take a copy print and go round all the cobblers in the district. You can start in the town. If our man's local, chances are he buys his footwear local. If we don't get any luck then try

The Man at the Walpole Bay Hotel

Ramsgate and Broadstairs. That'll do for a start. Now ... ,' Page broke off; his attention had been drawn elsewhere. Another car had pulled up at the hotel. Two women got out and were heading in his direction with a determination that suggested they were coming to see what was going on.

'... Those two look like a couple of nosey parkers if ever I saw them,' Page said disparagingly. 'I hope word hasn't got out. Don't let them too close, Constable. Don't want them trampling their dainty little toes over everything.'

Dorothy Coates was not there to be nosey, contrary to what Page had assumed. She had actually not heard anything about the incident on the clifftop; she had seen the brief mention there had been of it in the local newspaper, but that was all. She was simply taking her friend Effie Dalrymple out for a jaunt in her new motor, a Vauxhall Prince Henry of some four litres.

'She is a proper flyer!' she had shouted to Effie above the roar of the wind, as they had managed to record 72 mph along the Eastern Esplanade.

'Really Dorothy,' Effie said once they had slowed on the approach to the hotel. 'Don't you think that was a bit fast for the Esplanade?'

'She will do more than that,' Dorothy laughed as they got out at the hotel. 'The maker's brochure says the torpedo model is the fastest touring machine on the market. It has been tested at Brooklands at one hundred miles per hour you know.'

Effie smiled nervously, 'I hope you are not contemplating trying the same.'

'No, not really, though it does sound fun.' Dorothy looked at her watch. 'Hmm, bit early for cocktails. Pity. Oh, I say, look, some policemen. What do you suppose they are doing over there? Shall we go and see?'

As they approached the gathering the constable stepped forward to meet them. 'Right ladies, stand well away, please.'

Page took a pace towards them. 'This is the scene of a crime, ladies,' he said patronisingly. 'I must ask you to move on. There is nothing here to interest you.'

'Oh, to the contrary,' Dorothy objected, straining to get a better view of the forensic men at work. 'I am sure we should find the whole thing fascinating. Was it a crime of violence, Sergeant?'

'Inspector, madam; I'm not a sergeant. DI Archie Page. You may have read my name in the newspapers.'

'Yes, indeed. My apologies for reducing your rank, Detective Inspector.'

'Accepted, madam. Now if you and your friend would just move along. We are conducting an investigation into a serious crime. There may be clues hereabouts. You may unwittingly disturb something.'

'A serious crime? Would this be the death of poor Mr Grayson that we read about in the papers?'

'Indeed, madam, and who are you?'

'Dorothy Coates, Inspector.'

'I see, and were you acquainted with the deceased?'

'No, no. Just curious. I find crime quite fascinating. You policemen are *so* clever.'

'Yes, *so clever*,' Effie chorused.

Page looked gratified. 'Thank you, ladies. We try our best. Now if you would be so kind as to move along.'

Dorothy Coates inclined her head a little, in deference to the request. 'Of course,' she smiled. 'Let us go, Effie. That breeze is freshening, don't you think. It could come on to rain.'

Page waved at the two as they walked away. 'Ladies interested in crime, indeed,' he shrugged, looking over to the DC. 'Been reading too many Penny Dreadfuls, I dare say.'

The constable laughed.

They had walked less than fifty yards when Dorothy stopped. She bent down and picked up a discarded cigarette packet. 'Now that's unusual, Effie. Camel. That is an American brand of cigarette I believe. What do you think?' She held out the packet to her friend.

'Very nice.'

'A pretty design – but what's it doing here? Tourists, do you suppose? We don't get many Americans in Margate.'

Dorothy studied the packet for a moment, then put it into her handbag. 'We should go, Effie. I think it will rain shortly. Why don't we pay a visit to the Walpole Bay. It will soon be a suitable hour for a little refreshment – and I want to return Lucinda's bird book. She let me borrow it; most interesting the number of wading birds we have here along the coast.

Chapter 7

Deception

As they climbed the steps to the front entrance of the Walpole Bay Hotel a man emerged. He walked rapidly down, pushing rudely past an elderly couple who were taking their time, then walked urgently off towards the seafront.

'How rude, what an uncouth ruffian,' Effie said indignantly. 'Really, some people have no manners.'

'Yes,' Dorothy agreed. She paused her stride and allowed her gaze to follow the man as he headed in the direction of the beach. 'I think we've seen him before. Wasn't he on the pier when we went to see the *Margate Queen* cast off. You know, the one talking with that foreigner.'

'Foreigner? You mean the American man? Are Americans foreigners?' Effie frowned. 'Yes,' she said, answering her own question, 'I suppose they are. Funny, I never think of Americans as foreigners – but, of course, they are really. I think

The Man at the Walpole Bay Hotel

he was the other man. What's he doing in a good class of hotel like this?'

'Tradesman, quite probably. Ah, there's Simpson. We should ask him. Concierges know everything that's going on.'

'What a good idea.'

The concierge smiled politely as they approached, giving a slight semblance of a bow with his head. 'Ladies, good afternoon,' he made an exaggerated glance at his watch, 'or rather early evening I should perhaps say.'

'It is cocktail hour, Simpson,' Effie said smiling.

'Indeed madam, if you go through to the lounge, I shall send in Herbert, our new waiter, to look after you.'

Dorothy nodded. 'Thank you. Simpson, who was that rough-looking man who just left in such an unseemly hurry? Do you know?'

'No, Mrs Coates. I did challenge him when he came in earlier. He said he had a package for one of the guests.'

'Did he say which guest?'

Simpson shook his head gravely. 'He did not, Mrs Coates.'

Dorothy was on the verge of asking more but the moment was interrupted when two men walked in.'

'Inspector!' Dorothy waved. Page nodded politely in her direction, then went to the reception counter.

'What's he doing here?' Effie whispered as they went through to the lounge.

The Man at the Walpole Bay Hotel

'Probably the same as us, dear; come in for a drink before going home. He's probably had a challenging day, poor man.'

Effie looked a little perplexed. 'I thought they weren't supposed to drink on duty.'

'Never mind, sit down. Ah here's Herbert.'

The waiter came to where they had sunk into two comfortable armchairs. 'What is it to be, ladies, the usual?'

'I shall have a Negroni,' Dorothy said. 'Can the barman make one, do you suppose?'

'I'm sure he can, Mrs Coates ... and for you, Mrs Dalrymple; what is your pleasure?'

'Oh, my usual gin and Italian please, Herbert. Dorothy, why are you not having a gin and It? You always have that.'

'Well, I've changed my mind, Effie. The salesman at the motor agency made a Negroni for me, compliments of the Vauxhall Motor Company for all new customers. Cocktails are in these days, you know. They say it's the New York influence. That and the craze for jazz music and night clubs. I can't say I'm too fond of jazz – I'll just stick with the cocktails. Not everything that comes out of America is bad, though.'

Effie looked doubtful at that. 'Well, perhaps so, but there are gangs and murder too. I've heard in New York you can arrange to have someone bumped off for as little as ten dollars. Shocking.'

Dorothy was about to reply when she went quiet. She thought for a moment. 'Well, I wonder,' she eventually said.

The Man at the Walpole Bay Hotel

Effie waited in anticipation of her friend's thoughts, but instead all that came was Herbert, arriving with their drinks. 'I'm sorry to have kept you waiting, ladies,' he apologised, 'I was held up by that police inspector in the reception. He's questioning the staff about the burglary.'

'Burglary?' Dorothy gave him a quizzical stare. 'What burglary is that? Explain.'

'Of course, you would not know. It only happened this afternoon. One of the guests had her room broken into.'

'I say, that's pretty awful. Was she local?'

Herbert stuttered and looked awkward. 'Well, well, err, yes and no. Sort of. It was your niece's room, Mrs Coates – Miss Lucinda's.'

'Oh, poor girl. Where is she now?'

'In the reception lobby – with that inspector. Shall I let her know you're here?'

'Thank you, Herbert, no. Effie and I will go through to her in just a minute. When we've had a little tipple of our drinks.'

'You know, Effie,' Dorothy said. 'I think there could be more going on here in Margate than meets the eye.'

'Do you think so?'

'I do, Effie, I do. Now, drink up, and let's go and see what the good Inspector Page has to say for himself.'

Page and his DC were standing at the reception counter, questioning the concierge and the receptionist. Standing close to him, Lucinda listened attentively. She turned as the two women entered the lobby.

'Aunt Dorothy,' she called on seeing them. 'Have you heard? My room has been burgled.'

Page was momentarily fazed by the new arrivals. He shot a hostile glance at the interruption from Dorothy. 'If you don't mind, ladies, this is a private matter.'

'It's all right, Inspector,' Lucinda butted in, 'this lady is my aunt.'

Page made a slight puffing noise. 'Very well, miss. As I was saying, there seems to be nothing missing from your belongings – is that so?'

'Yes, Inspector, that is correct.'

Page thought for a moment. 'Then there really is no crime to report, miss. Unless the hotel management wish to press on the matter of a trespass. Clearly the intruder was disturbed before he could take anything.'

Effie raised a diffident hand. 'Are we sure it was a man, Inspector?'

Page half closed his eyes and briefly glanced up at the ceiling. 'It usually is, madam. Don't get a lot of lady felons. Very rare in my experience.'

'What about that rough-looking fellow who ran out of the hotel as we came in, Simpson?' Dorothy cocked an eyebrow at the concierge.

'Who was this, then?' The Inspector interrupted.

'A very suspicious-looking fellow,' Effie responded. 'Not at all the sort you would expect in a quality hotel like this.'

Page turned to the concierge. 'Do you know anything about it?'

The Man at the Walpole Bay Hotel

'A tradesman, I believe, Inspector. Delivering a package to one of the guests.'

'Do we know who was the recipient?'

'As I said before to the ladies, I'm afraid we do not, Inspector.'

'So, there we have it, ladies, a delivery boy.' Page turned sharply away to a man making his way towards the exit. 'Don't leave, please, Mr Donovan. I haven't finished with you yet.'

The man turned back and joined the group. 'This is Mr Donovan, Aunt,' Lucinda said. 'He heard the burglar and went to take a look. He must have disturbed him, which is probably why there was nothing taken. Harry, this is my Aunt Dorothy and her friend Effie Dalrymple.'

Donovan removed his hat. 'Most pleased to make your acquaintance, ladies.'

'Tell me, Mr Donovan, or may I call you Harry?'

'Please do.'

'What sort of noise alerted you, Harry?'

Page became impatient. 'If you don't mind ladies, this is confidential police business. Why don't you take your niece and go and have a nice cup of tea, or something – in the lounge. I have some questions to put to this gentleman.'

'Oh, we don't mind, Inspector,' Effie beamed. 'We find it most interesting – don't we, Dorothy.'

'Confidential, ladies, confidential,' Page said, a note of irritation rising in his voice. 'Now, if you don't mind.'

The Man at the Walpole Bay Hotel

Dorothy shrugged off the remark. 'Of course. Lucinda, Effie.' She gestured in the direction of the lounge. 'Shall we?'

In the lounge Dorothy prepared to sink down into a buttoned leather armchair. 'Oh, I quite forgot in all that hubbub, I wanted to return this, Lucinda.' Dorothy pulled the bird book from her handbag. 'Most interesting, dear. Now, it's too late for tea, and one should only take coffee at the finish of luncheon or dinner – a cocktail is called for, I think. That is definitely appropriate for the hour. Lucinda, dear, see if you can find Herbert, there's a good girl.'

When Lucinda returned she had Harry by her side. 'Would you mind awfully if Harry joins us, Aunt Dorothy?' she said. 'I thought I'd offer him a drink. Inspector Page has finished with him for the time being, and it seems the least I can do after he obviously scared off that burglar.'

'Of course, do join us, Harry. What would you like? Herbert, would you get something for Mr Donovan here. Now do tell us what happened.'

'Yes, please do,' Effie chorused.

'There's not a lot to tell. I didn't do anything particularly courageous. I heard this loud thump coming from Miss Lucinda's room and went to investigate. The door was shut so I knocked and just called out, are you all right in there.'

'Ooh,' Effie said, a note of shock in her voice. 'and what happened? Was there a reply?'

The Man at the Walpole Bay Hotel

'No, so I went back to my room. Then I heard what sounded like someone running in the corridor. I went to take a look but there was no one. It was then I noticed the bedroom door was hanging open, so I went to investigate. The room was a dreadful mess. That's when Miss Lucinda turned up.'

'Yes, at first I thought Harry was the burglar,' Lucinda smiled at Donovan. 'He went and alerted the hotel staff. I'm so grateful for that, Harry.'

'Oh, not a bit. It was nothing. Delighted to be of assistance,' he said. Then his eyes caught sight of the bird book. 'May I,' he requested, and picked it up without waiting for a reply.

'It is most interesting and informative, Harry,' Dorothy said with enthusiasm. 'I have had the loan of it myself these past two days.'

Donovan flicked through the pages, glancing briefly at the illustrations, then replaced it on the table. 'Well,' he said, after finishing his drink and looking deliberately at his watch. 'I have an appointment so I shall have to leave you, ladies. Dinner at eight,' he winked at Lucinda then smiled at Dorothy. 'Your niece has agreed to dine as my guest this evening. There's a rather good restaurant near to the harbour. I wish you a pleasant evening, ladies.'

'I'll meet you here in the lobby at eight,' Lucinda called after him. 'I must go Aunt Dorothy, I have errands to run.'

'What a personable young man,' Dorothy said after Lucinda had left them.

The Man at the Walpole Bay Hotel

Effie's voice broke into a suppressed giggle. 'Do you suppose he's taken bit of a shine to our Lucy?'

'I suspect he has ... and why not, she really is a rather pretty girl. Now, shall we dine here or go into the town?'

'Here I think.'

'In that case we should ask Herbert to refresh our drinks.'

'Good idea,' Effie concurred

*

'Morning, Seymour.' Donovan pulled up a chair at Trevelyan's table, where he took a slice of toast from the rack and poured himself a cup of tea.

'Why is it, Harry, that you always have to interrupt my breakfast? It really isn't on, dear boy.'

Donovan grinned broadly. 'Good point, not so sure myself, Seymour. Quality of tea here isn't up to much — and the toast at my place has more crunch about it too.'

'Hmm, so what do we know?'

'The peelers were around at the Walpole Bay. That flatfoot Page. I think he's got me in is sights.'

'Has he now.' Seymour Trevelyan seemed unmoved by the news. 'And why would that be, do you suppose? Hmm.'

'That man, Grayson; the one who took a dive off the cliffs up at Botany Bay. From the line of questioning I'd say he's putting me in the frame. Trying me for size, to see if I fit. I don't think it's more than the policeman's intuition but it could be awkward. Anything we can do?'

'Wouldn't be wise at this stage. Life is already complicated enough. We'll just have to ride it out and keep a low profile.

'There's another problem – I think.'

'Think?'

'Could be a coincidence. The girl. Someone turned her room over.'

'Looking for?'

'Same thing we are – I think.'

'Don't keep telling me what you *think*, dear boy, tell me what you *know*.'

Donovan bit into his toast and chewed noisily. 'I took the girl out to dinner last night. It was useful. She told me an interesting story.' Donovan paused again, this time to drink his tea.

'Which was?'

'She was in the British Museum Library. A couple of boyos came in acting strangely. They chased after a man who had been in there going through the books. I think that man was Ernst.'

'Thinking again, Harry?'

'Okay, it's a hunch. But look at it this way. Ernst and I had a rendezvous at the Museum. He must have known he was being followed so it looks like he dodged into the museum library. What if he shoved the document into a book, just for safekeeping, while he threw the others off, with the intention of going back to collect it later … but they caught up with him in Kensington – and did for him. Now if you could get one of your lads in London to go and take a look …'

The Man at the Walpole Bay Hotel

Trevelyan's expression was dour. 'Risky. If we're seen poking around it could raise alarms. Have you any idea what section Ernst was likely to have been in?'

'Well now, here's more speculation, but bear with it, Seymour. Ornithology.'

'Ah, your pretty young lady's pet subject.'

'Precisely. She has a book from the library with her. Maybe it's *the* book. What if the boyos think what I'm thinking, and they broke into her room looking for it?'

'Has she still got it?'

'Yes, she'd loaned it to her aunt. I managed to get a quick thumb through it.'

'And?'

'Not there ... but she did let drop she had borrowed two books.'

'So where's the other one?' Donovan shrugged. Trevelyan flapped his arms with an air of frustration. 'Well, start looking. Maybe it's in neither of her books. I'll see what can be done about somebody in London to pay a visit to the museum library.'

Chapter 8

Useful information

It was a little after nine in the morning when the elegantly pointed nose of the Prince Henry came to a halt outside a fine house. It was well situated in a desirable location, overlooking Palm Bay. Dorothy got out of the car, opened the gate and walked up the path to the front door, on which she knocked loudly. After a short interval an upstairs window was opened and Effie Dalrymple poked her head out. 'Hold on,' she called out, 'Freida's day off. I'll come down and let you in.'

'I must find a maid like Freida,' Dorothy said when the front door was opened. 'She's such a treasure. Muggers is a good enough housekeeper, but being without a maid is not at all satisfactory. The last girl was dreadfully sloppy. Not at all like Freida.'

'Ah, but Freida's old school, you see; that's the difference. Dear Max found her. God rest him. She was with us in Berlin when we were first married.'

The Man at the Walpole Bay Hotel

'Yes, Berlin, that's what I came to talk to you about. You speak German, don't you?'

'Of course, I married a German man; I *had* to learn it. It would have been impossible to manage the house otherwise; all those receptions. Even Freida spoke nothing but German then. We spent the first four years of our married life in Berlin. What a lovely city. So many memories. I loved the Tiergarten and our walks together. Such happy days. All changed now, though. Wilhelm is not like the old Kaiser; and as for all this talk of war, it doesn't bear thinking about.'

'Quite so, Effie. Now look at this.' Dorothy pulled two folded sheets of foolscap paper from her handbag.'

'What is it?'

'I don't know. I think it fell out of Lucy's bird book. I found it in my bag this morning. It's some kind of official document – but it's all in German. I thought perhaps you could read it for me.'

Effie took the sheets of paper and unfolded them flat on the table. She studied them for several minutes without comment. 'It's quite difficult, Dorothy, because it's written in legal language. Not the sort of thing you would use in conversation. I shall need to look out my dictionary. I can tell you this, though. It's come from the German Embassy in Washington and looks like the minutes of a meeting.'

Dorothy peered down onto the document. 'Now that *is* a most curious thing. Why don't you pop it into a safe place for the time being, and when you have a moment perhaps you could get out your

The Man at the Walpole Bay Hotel

dictionary and write down a sort of translation. It doesn't need to be terribly precise for the moment. Just enough for us to get the gist of the text.'

'Do you think it has anything to do with what's been going on? You know, the funny business over Lucy's break in?'

'I don't know, Effie, possibly, but I can't be sure until I can read it. I'm going down to the town in the Prince Henry; why don't you come with me? I want to go to the offices of the *Thanet Gazette*. Afterwards we can have our elevenses somewhere.'

'What do you want from the *Thanet Gazette*?'

'Weather, Effie. I want to know which way the wind was blowing three days ago.'

Effie looked perplexed. 'Why on earth would you wish to know that?'

'I'll tell you while we're on our way.'

'Well, I hope you're not going to drive like a woman possessed. You really have got the very bit between your teeth since you acquired that Prince Henry motor.'

'No, no, don't worry. We shall just poodle along with the hood down. The fresh air will do us good.'

'Well so long as you do. I don't want my hat blown off to be sent rolling down the Esplanade.'

'Not to worry. By the by, Lucy had a tremendous evening with her young man, Harry.'

'Is he – her young man, that is?'

'Rather seems it might be so. He took her to a splendid restaurant for a slap-up do.'

'I say, how romantic.'

The Man at the Walpole Bay Hotel

*

'How can I help you, ladies?' The clerk in the offices of the *Thanet Gazette* pulled a green celluloid eye-shade from his forehead and smiled at the two women.

'Would you have archive copies of the last three issues of the paper that we might see?' Dorothy asked.

The smile turned to an obliging grin as the clerk agreed they did. 'If you would care to wait a few moments I'll get someone to bring them up from the basement.' He lifted the telephone earpiece and tapped on the cradle it had been hanging on. 'Mary, could you please bring up the last three editions from the archive? We have visitors on reception who would like to see them.'

He replaced the earpiece and pointed to a table. 'Ladies, if you would like to sit at that table over there? Someone will bring the copies to you.' Minutes later a young woman came in through a side door and placed the papers in front of them.

'What are you looking for?' Effie's voice was low and conspiratorial, as if she were in some hallowed institution like a library or a church.

'The weather.' Dorothy turned the pages and inspected each issue. 'Just as I thought,' she said. Getting to her feet she took the papers to the clerk. 'Thank you. Come along Effie. We're all done here.'

'What did you find out?' Effie asked when they were outside in the street again.

The Man at the Walpole Bay Hotel

'That the wind was blowing north-westerly, Effie. On all three days.'

'Is that important?'

'Yes – I think it is. Right, police station next. I've arranged to meet Lucy there. She has to give her account of the burglary to the desk sergeant. I think after that it will just about be time for our elevenses. I thought we might go to the tearooms on the pier.'

*

The police station was a solid, unlovely building; as squat and ugly as the business conducted within its hard flint walls. It was a place of multiple functions. On the cold flagstones of the ground floor there was the town lock-up: four cramped cells secured behind heavy low doors. A stairway to the first floor opened into the more generous, though equally forbidding, courtroom. There was a dark wooden dais supporting the bench on which the local magistrates sat. It, too, was a room of more than one purpose: acting, when no court was in session, as the Town Council chamber.

Lucinda was already there when the two women arrived. She had given her statement to the sergeant and was talking with DI Page, who looked at them with not a little surprise. 'Hello ladies, what are you doing here?' he said as they stepped in through the front door.

'Meeting my niece, Inspector?'

Page gave all three women a look of irritable resignation. 'This is not the ladies waiting room on

The Man at the Walpole Bay Hotel

Waterloo Station, you know. Police business only to be conducted here.'

Dorothy tried her best to look contrite, and Effie muttered a reticent little 'Sorry, Inspector.'

'Apology accepted,' Page conceded. 'Seeing as how you're here, I was wanting to ask you some questions anyway.'

'About the break-in?'

'No, though I've just been talking to this young lady about her burglary. It seems something did go missing after all. A book; a book on birds; the property of the library of the British Museum, where she works. Quite a valuable book by all accounts.'

Dorothy frowned at that, but all she said was, 'How interesting.'

'If you say so, madam, though I'm more concerned with the events of last week. The night Mr Grayson went over the cliff – so to speak. You weren't in that vicinity, by any chance, were you?'

'No.'

'But you did subsequently visit the spot where the body was found. I should warn you; you were seen there.' Dorothy nodded.

'Was there any particular reason why you would want to visit the spot then?'

'Only curiosity, Inspector. I'd read about it. I wondered if the scene might offer any hint of how the incident had occurred – and, as it happens, I think it did. Would you like to hear it?'

'A bit of an amateur sleuth, are we, madam? Best leave it to us professionals. That's what we're paid for. We do, of course, appreciate the public's help – where they are able.' He turned to Lucinda. 'Right ho, miss, I think that's it. Thank you, ladies, off you go now, and I wish you a good day.'

Dorothy looked at her watch. 'I say, *tempus fugit;* midday. We've missed our elevenses, Effie; time for luncheon I'd say. The Prince Henry's parked just round the corner. Why don't we pop off to Botany Bay and get a spot of something at the Fayreness Hotel. You have time don't you, Lucy dear?'

'Of course ...,' Lucinda was saying, but she stopped short, pulling back on her aunt's arm. They were passing the Wellington Hotel and two men had come bursting noisily out through the bar door and made off rapidly, too deep in conversation to notice the three women.

Lucy drew in a sharp breath. 'I recognise those men. What are they doing here?' Her gaze followed the figures until they turned a corner and disappeared from sight. 'They were the same ones who were acting strangely in the Reading Room at the Library.'

'Are you sure?'

'Certain. They were as close to me as I am to you. They shoved past me so rudely in the library corridor they almost bowled me over. I won't forget *them* in a hurry.'

'We've seen one of them as well,' Effie said, looking at Dorothy. 'That's the one who rather brusquely pushed his way past that elderly couple coming out of the Walpole Bay. Is it not?'

The Man at the Walpole Bay Hotel

'I think you're right, Effie, and what is more, wasn't it the same one talking to that American boarding the paddler. I think this needs looking into.'

*

The Prince Henry came to a halt in front of the Fayreness Hotel; Lucinda and Effie both still clutching onto their hats.

Dorothy looked elated, grinning like a circus clown. 'The Prince fairly *flew* along the Esplanade, don't you think?'

'You're a bit of a tearaway, Aunt,' Lucinda admonished, laughing.

Effie looked mildly disapproving. 'Just don't let the constables catch you is all I can say, Dorothy. You'll be for the high jump if they do.'

'Oh, tush. Splendid motor. Flat out speed, that's what it was *made* for. Now, food. Why don't we go out onto the veranda. It's a lovely day; we can sit under a parasol and enjoy the view.'

Installed at their table, Effie waved an arm generally at the horizon. 'Now isn't this nice. Just the three of us and that lovely view of the cliffs. And nothing to spoil it ... except *that*!' Effie pointed an accusing finger at the object of her distaste. 'Dreadful. They shouldn't allow tramps like that up here. I ask you, what *does* he look like?'

Dorothy stood up. 'I know that face – and I want a word with *him*. Excuse me; I'll not be a minute.

The Man at the Walpole Bay Hotel

If the waiter comes I'll have the plate of the day, so long as it's not pork. Otherwise I'll have the fish. Back in a jiffy.' Dorothy made off in the direction of her quarry. 'Ratty,' she said affably when she reached him. 'May I have a word?'

The man she addressed had a shabby, grimy appearance. His coat was patched and his trousers showed neglect of the laundry. His face had a three-day growth of grey stubble; yellowy brown stained from the tobacco he chewed and the spittle he let dribble across it. But for all this, he pulled a solid gold double hunter from his waistcoat pocket.

'Allo, Mrs Coates, and a fine good morning to yer.' He flipped the watch cover open and grinned a display of gold capped teeth. 'Well, praps it ain't no longer morning, missus … but good day to you anyway. 'Ow can I 'elp?'

'Murder, Ratty. I think there's been a murder.'

'Oh, yeah, missus. 'Ow's that then?'

'You heard about Mr Grayson?'

'Who 'asn't, I ask you. Very suspicious, I'd say.'

'And why would you say that, Ratty? Any word out there – perhaps?'

'Well now, Mrs Coates, and seein as it's you like – no, no one's sayin nuffin. But I might'a saw things. Out there, that night like.'

'Did you now?'

'I did.'

'And what was it you saw?'

'I was 'ere that night. Wiv my old lurcher, Toby. There were this cove. Very smart 'ee were.

The Man at the Walpole Bay Hotel

Dressed all fancy. Mind you, clothes don't make the man and I gotta say 'ee looked like a wrongun ta me. Sat dahn at a table 'ee were. That Mr Grayson, 'ee goes over and starts yarnin wiv 'im, talking abaht birds they was. I know cos I walked past 'em, didn't I; took old Toby for 'is constitutional. We walked just ter the Captain Digby then come back. On account of 'ow old Toby 'ees gettin on and 'ee don't have much wind these days, poor bugger. When we was passin that old flint fort, I see somink. Some geyser were walking away from the cliff, weren't they. It weren't the one talking ter Grayson in the pub. It were another geyser. All in an 'urry like, ee was. Right from where that Grayson got 'imself tipped over.'

'Aha. Sure it wasn't the man Mr Grayson had been talking to earlier?'

Ratty Bumstead screwed up the stubble on his face. 'Could'a bin, 'ard ta say. It were dark, weren't it. One fing, though, 'ee ad a light coloured 'at on. That showed up in the dark.'

'What sort of hat?'

'Difficult, missus. Could 'av been a Skimmer or somink like that. Not a wide brim thing, though.'

'A Panama, perhaps?'

'Could be, 'ard to say – but I don't fink so.'

'Anything else?'

'Not really, missus. Can't fink why anyone would want to shove that Grayson over the top.'

'It *is* strange, I grant you. Thank you, Ratty. You know you really ought to report this to the constabulary. There's an Inspector Page from

The Man at the Walpole Bay Hotel

Dover in charge. He's at the town lock-up this very moment.

'So I 'erd. I'll not go near that bugger, though. Constables ain't my cuppa, Mrs Coates. I'll wish you a good day now.'

'Who was that?' Lucinda said, when Dorothy resumed her place at the table.

'Ratty Bumstead. Local character; potty as shrimp paste, mind you, though he is a man with his ear to the ground. And not as dotty as he appears. You could be excused for thinking he looks like he hasn't a penny to bless himself – but don't let that fool you. Probably the richest man in Margate; quite possibly the county. Rag-and-bone man. Made a fortune out of the South African war. He bought up all the old Martini rifles when the army changed to new ones – so they say. That and a very large consignment of tinned Mafeking pudding. It was on a steamer bound for Cape Town when the war ended. Rumour is he sold the whole lot, pudding *and* guns, to a dealer in Tangier.'

Effie waved a hand in disapproval. 'A doubtful scoundrel, Lucy dear. A ne'er-do-well of the local underworld.'

'Nonsense, Effie. Ratty knows people, that's all. The lower orders trust him, so he gets to hear their gossip. Never mind, here's the waiter. I think perhaps a little white wine with the luncheon. They do a very good Riesling.'

Chapter 9

Red herrings

The house in Westbrook had a fine sea view, though that was not what had recommended it to George Coates. The advantage was its coach house; not large, but sufficient for the pony and trap he had used for his visits to the homes of his patients. When Dr Coates passed away, his widow Dorothy had no need of the facility. The upkeep of a stable lad and forage for a pony was an expense she wished to shed, and so she did, availing herself of one of Margate's numerous hackney carriages when she had need of transport.

George had passed away five years after the old queen, Victoria. That was in 1906; but by 1914, the world had changed. The modern fashion was the motorcar, and the horse had been largely relegated to pulling commercial carts. For those who could not run to the cost of a motorcar, there was now the option of the motor omnibus.

The Man at the Walpole Bay Hotel

Dorothy had quickly taken to the new invention and so, once again, the coach house served a purpose: home to her handsome Vauxhall Prince Henry sporting torpedo – a motor of some elegance and a good turn of speed.

The table in the conservatory was littered with scraps of paper; little pages torn from a notebook, each one carrying a few scribbled words. There was that American boarding the paddler for London and the curious clips of conversation she and Effie had overheard; a mystery in its own right. And what about the man he was talking to – and Irishman? Perhaps. He had been seen rushing out of the Walpole Bay Hotel at the same time Lucy's room had been burgled ... and why steal her bird book? That didn't make sense – or did it? And everything revolved around the prostrate body of Benedict Grayson – lying at the bottom of the cliffs at Botany Bay – or did it? Maybe none of these things were connected, maybe they were all just red herrings?

Dorothy sat looking at the fragments of paper, touching on each one randomly with her fingers, pushing their order around, trying to create a pattern. It was emerging, but it was not giving her the answers she wanted. This detecting business was proving to be more complicated than she had imagined.

In the middle of her task she was interrupted; the telephone in the sitting room rang. When she picked up the receiver, the voice in her ear sounded excited. 'Dorothy, is that you?'

'Well, if it isn't I'm being burgled.'
'Oh dear, Dorothy, I do hope not.'
'No, no, what is it Effie?'
'I found time to translate that paper. You know, the one you left with me. The one in dreadfully proper German.'
'And what did you find?'
'You won't believe what it says. I didn't myself – I had to go back and check it again.'
'Well, why don't you tell me?'
'Over the telephone? Is that safe? The operator could be listening. Yours is not a party line, is it?'
'No. George insisted we were not to share the line with another subscriber; confidentiality of patients, you see.'
'Well, I really do think we should meet.'
'We should, Effie. I'll drive over to you; that will be quickest.'

To the accompaniment of the Prince Henry's exhaust burbling along Marine Drive, Dorothy applied her mind to the notes she had assembled on the conservatory table. Passing the harbour master's office, she could just see the pier where the London-bound paddler embarked its passengers. It again recalled to her mind the snatch of conversation she and Effie had overheard. The strange reference to the wrong man. It might have passed unnoticed in the normal course of events, but this was *not* normal. Lucy had seen one of the men before; acting strangely in the British Museum Library. None of it was adding up, the whole business nagged at her mind.

The Man at the Walpole Bay Hotel

Going up Fort Hill she speculated on what Effie's translation might tell her. She was becoming sure it must be connected, though she could not see how. As she passed the newly built Winter Gardens she caught sight of a news vendor's placard: RUSSIA MOBILISES, it bannered, *Pledge to Support Serbia*. Next to it, another placard announced ULSTER VOLOUNTEER FORCE IN ARMED CLASH WITH IRISH VOLUNTEERS.

A light went on in Dorothy's mind. 'How interesting,' she said under her breath, 'I wonder.' No, she said mentally. It is not good practice to jump to conclusions.

Freida answered the front doorbell. She half nodded to Dorothy in the German fashion of her training as a servant. 'Good morning, Madam Coates. Mrs Dalrymple is waiting for you in the withdrawing room.'

She ushered Dorothy through to the back of the house and into the drawing room, where Effie was sitting reading the morning newspaper. 'It is such unsettling news. Do you suppose there will be war, Dorothy?'

'I fear it is inevitable, Effie. Now, what have we with this translation?'

'Here it is.' Effie handed over a neatly typed sheet.

'Fenians,' Dorothy said slowly, having read and reread it. 'How very interesting.'

The Man at the Walpole Bay Hotel

After a moment or two of thought, she stood up. 'Right, there is something we must do. I'll tell you on the way.'

Effie looked slightly put out by the haste. 'But I've asked cook to prepare a little cold luncheon for us,' she protested.

'Later, Effie. If it's cold it will keep, whereas this will not. Come along.'

'Where to?'

'First, the ticket office of the Queen Line Steamers. Then to Messrs Thomas Cooke & Co. There are enquiries to be made.'

In the ticket office of the Queen Line company, Dorothy put her question. 'Do you keep a record of passengers who buy tickets?'

The clerk shook his head, a look of disinterest on his face. 'No madam, we do not.'

'What about foreigners?'

The clerk's head continued to shake, his lips pursed in a very negative fashion. 'Sorry. Was there any special reason?'

'Yes – but I can't tell you. It's an investigation.'

The clerk furrowed his brow. He looked sceptical; the two women in front of him seemed unlikely detectives – and were certainly not from the police. 'Investigation?' The tone was truculent. 'What kind of investigation?'

'Confidential.'

He shrugged. 'Sorry, can't help?'

'What if I told you it was a man running off after leaving a lady compromised?'

The Man at the Walpole Bay Hotel

The clerk remained insolently uncooperative. 'Madam, even if he was running off with the crown jewels I couldn't help. Good day, ladies.'

Disappointed, they turned to go, but before they got to the door he called after them, this time in a more conciliatory voice. 'Unless the passenger had luggage, that is. We keep a record of that, so the right person gets the right bag at the end of the journey.'

The two turned to face the clerk, then marched resolutely back to his station. 'He was a foreigner, an American. Does that help?' Dorothy said hopefully.

The clerk pulled a vellum-bound ledger from beneath the counter. He opened the book. 'When?'

'Last Friday. The midday sailing.'

The clerk turned to the relevant page and ran his hand down it, finally tapping his index finger on an entry. 'Only one American. A Mr Jackson Molloy, Boston, Massachusetts.'

'Wonderful.' Dorothy dived a hand into her reticule and produced a florin. 'For your troubles,' she smiled.

The clerk returned the smile and dropped the coin into his pocket. 'A pleasure, ladies.'

'What a stroke of good luck,' Dorothy said as they left the ticket office. 'Come on, we can leave the Prince Henry here and go on foot to the town.'

'Irish-American, I'll be bound,' she added, as they made their way to the Thomas Cooke offices. 'I smell Fenians, Effie.'

The Man at the Walpole Bay Hotel

The offices of Messrs Thomas Cooke, travel agent, were fronted by the plate-glass window of a shop and adorned with well-illustrated posters showing exotic destinations. Inside, a young woman in a high-collared lace blouse guided them to a table with comfortable chairs set around it. She was immediately followed by a well-dressed young man who joined them round the table.

'If I wanted to go to Boston, from where would I sail?' Dorothy asked.

'Southampton to New York, madam. From there by railroad. There is an excellent service.'

'Hmm,' Dorothy hesitated over her next question and how to pose it. Cooke's had a reputation for discretion and she was not sure if they would be willing to assist. 'If I wished to find out if a certain person were travelling on such a route, how would I go about that?'

The young man seemed totally unperturbed by the enquiry. 'Very simple, madam. One would only have to consult the ship's manifest. It is a public document. Are you seeking someone in particular?'

'I am. Are you able to help me?'

The young man widened his eyes, as if in astonishment. 'Of course, madam. We are here to help. That is the ethos of this company. Politeness and helpfulness. They are our watchwords.'

'That was surprisingly easy, Effie,' Dorothy said, feeling the warm flush of success. 'I think we are making progress. Now we should go back to your house for that luncheon. We mustn't upset cook.'

The Man at the Walpole Bay Hotel

*

When Inspector Page had arrived to investigate the death of Benedict Grayson he had found the Margate police station to be cramped. The only office available for Page was quite small and there was not enough space for the DC he had co-opted to assist in the investigation. Walter Godley had to be content with something not much larger than a broom cupboard further along the corridor.

Detective Sergeant Grist, the officer who normally headed all criminal investigations in the town, was on leave of sickness, and it was his office Page had now co-opted. There had also once been an inspector at Margate, but he too was absent, having moved on to another station. So, it was a small force and close knit; the intrusion of a renowned prima donna in the guise of Archie Page had caused a certain amount of friction – particularly as he had taken over DS Grist's desk. Should Grist return during the course of Page's investigation, the DS would find he had been displaced to the cramped confines of the basement, a windowless room next to the coal cellar.

In the front hall, just inside the public entrance, there was an enquiries desk manned by a senior constable who sat behind a solid counter, together with the station sergeant.

Finally, there was a large muster room for the duty constables, and next to that a small tearoom –

The Man at the Walpole Bay Hotel

though, as often as not the senior staff preferred a café across the square from the gaol.

Page looked up from the latest report he was scrutinising. 'There is one common thread here, Godley,' he announced to the DC, 'and that's our man, Henry Donovan. He's a man we need to know more about, and I think I need another talk with that waiter up at the Fayreness Hotel. While I'm up there see what you can find out about Donovan – you might profit from a call to Scotland Yard. Let's check up on his address in London. See if anything comes out of that.'

*

It was Monday and the day was fine. 'August bank holiday,' Dorothy said down the phone to her friend. 'We should go out for a jolly.'

Outside Effie Dalrymple's house, the Prince Henry stood with its engine purring. Dorothy hooted three times on the klaxon, the pre-arranged signal for Effie to join her.
   'We should go to the beach,' Effie said, with the enthusiasm of a child. 'I do love the beach with its awnings and deckchairs. It always looks *so* gay in the summer. We should take advantage of this glorious weather while we can.'

When they arrived in the town it was thronging with people, all promenading in their Sunday best. Dorothy parked the Prince Henry close to the

The Man at the Walpole Bay Hotel

harbour master's office and from there they walked arm in arm along the promenade.

Close to the town clock, overlooking the sands, the band of the Queen's Own Royal West Kent Regiment were playing a repertoire of stirring marches. The two women stopped. 'Splendid band,' Dorothy was saying, but she was cut short and interrupted by Effie.

'Now what do think of that?' Effie pointed to where two men were standing in conversation with a third.

Dorothy raised a hand to shade her eyes. 'Where?'

'There. That ghastly tramp fellow, Bumstead ... and aren't those other two with him the ones Lucy said she'd seen before in the library in London?'

'You know, Effie, I do believe you are right. Now, what are they up to, do you suppose?'

They watched them for a while, until the group split up, each man going his own way.

'Very odd that. Come on.' Dorothy took Effie by the arm. 'I'd like an ice cream. Look, there's a cart over there.'

'You know,' Effie said, as they walked along the water's edge, boots removed and paddling their toes in the cool salt water, 'I can't help thinking that old tramp knows a lot more than he's letting on.'

'My thoughts too. Listen ...,' Dorothy held up a finger; the town clock began to chime the half hour, '... twelve thirty. We should find a little luncheon somewhere. How about the Fayreness?

The Man at the Walpole Bay Hotel

They have a new chef: Monsieur Janeau, a Frenchman – from Paris, I believe. I hear he's awfully good.'

*

As they entered the Fayreness hotel, Dorothy nodded in the direction of the reception desk. 'Oh look, isn't that Inspector Page?'

She walked briskly over to where the Inspector was occupied questioning the waiter. He stopped when he saw the two women. From the strained look on his face it was clear their presence was not what he wanted.

'Inspector, do you have a moment? I would like a word with you, if that is convenient.'

Page struggled to preserve a decorous stance. The smile he gave her was more of a grimace. 'I'm afraid I'm rather busy, ladies. Perhaps some other time.'

'There's no hurry, Inspector,' Effie smiled. 'We're here for our luncheon. Are you lunching here too?'

'No, madam, I'm here to ask questions of this waiter.'

'Well, perhaps when you have finished?' Dorothy queried. 'You see, I have a theory which I would very much like to share with you.'

Page wrung what was a barely perceptible smile from his face. 'Very interesting, ladies, I'm sure. However, I must get back to the station. I know you wish to be helpful but you must leave it to the professionals. I can assure you, the investigation is in good hands. Enjoy your lunch, and a very good day to you both.'

'It's a shame that he is in such a hurry,' Effie commented as they made their way to their table.

'Probably got the policeman's tiffin waiting for him.'

'Is that any good – a policeman's tiffin?'

'Shouldn't think so, Dorothy chuckled. 'George used to tell me that when he was Chief Medical Officer for the colonial police in Delhi, well, the lunchtime tiffin was dreadful. Mostly rice – and a few doubtful vegetables. Mind you, the subedar-major was a Sikh, and many of them don't eat meat, you know.'

'Is that so? Well, it's a good job the Inspector isn't in India then. I hope he gets more than rice down at the police station.'

'It is more likely to be bread and cheese, Effie.'

'Well, I hope he gets some pudding, at least. He looks a bit underfed, you know. Now, what do you think about those two men with Bumstead? *I* think you are right; they could be Fenians.'

'Yes, things are pointing in that direction, Effie. In which case I would rather like to know what they were talking about with Ratty.

*

Back at the lockup, DC Godley had just returned from the café on the other side of the square. 'Any news, sir? Did the waiter know anything?'

'He did. Not a great deal, but one thing is confirmed: the last person to see Grayson alive was Donovan. They were seen talking together – and they both left the hotel at the same time.'

Page sat down at his desk. 'What's this?' He waved a typewritten sheet at Godley.

'Report on Donavan, sir. As far as I could ascertain he does not seem to have a regular employ, so to speak.'

'Bit of a dilettante is he?'

'Would seem that way, sir. Bit of a ladies man by the little I could uncover. Very secretive man too.'

'Gigolo, eh. Naughty, naughty.'

'He's not short of the spondoolics by the look of it. Very posh address in London. Kensington.'

Page raised an eyebrow. 'Very fashionable. Can't be cheap. So where does he get his subsistence then?'

'Well, there doesn't seem to be any family to speak of. Mother and father both passed on. Small time gentry; farmers but not rich as far as I could see. Father married into a banking family but I don't think much was inherited in their direction.

'So, how does our Mr Donovan earn his crust?'

'More than a crust, sir. What with an address like that; and staying at the Walpole Bay Hotel; that's not exactly the pauper's workhouse.'

'So, where's the money coming from, Constable Godley? Flattering old ladies – or young heiresses?'

'Or perhaps taking commissions to dispose of awkward situations - like pushing men over cliffs, sir?'

'Godley, see if you can find out if there was any connection between the two of them. Maybe Donovan stood to gain financially from Grayson's death. A will, perhaps? Or could it be that you're right and Donovan was paid to do it? Let's see if Grayson had enemies. Maybe he was putting the squeeze on someone.'

'Blackmail? That's nasty.'

Page clucked his tongue. 'It happens, Godley. Even the most respectable toffs have skeletons hidden away. In fact, Godley, in the opinion of this humble policeman, the toffier they are, the more bodies there are hidden. Get your shovel out and start digging. Go to it lad.'

Chapter 10

Arrest

The morning paper always arrived in time for breakfast. Dorothy Coates liked to read her copy of *The Times* as she crunched her way through the toast, dipping strips of it into a softly boiled egg. The headline was clear.

GREAT BRITAIN DECLARES WAR ON GERMANY!

That was going to ruin the rest of what the government had announced as an extended August bank holiday.
Mobilisation of reservists to aid France and Belgium. Nation urged to be alert for spies, it went on to warn. It was what she had expected. It was what everyone had expected, ever since July when the Germans had demanded free passage for its armies to invade France – and Belgium had refused.

The Man at the Walpole Bay Hotel

On the same front page, but relegated to the bottom right-hand corner, there was the picture of a rather nondescript man. Under the picture the caption read *Ernst Weber, German diplomat reported missing.* It went on,

> *Herr Weber, an employee of the German civil service, has been reported as missing by the German Embassy in London. This reporter has discovered that Herr Weber is employed by that country's embassy in Washington, and may have been at large in London on a mission of spying. He was reportedly last seen in the area of the British Museum. Any member of the public knowing of his whereabouts should report it directly to the nearest constabulary.*

'I am going out, Muggers,' Dorothy informed her housekeeper, Mrs Muggeridge, when she had finished her breakfast. 'I shall not be back for luncheon.'

Suitably attired for driving, in a summer weight dark blue cotton twill coat, with a double breasted front, she went to the coach house. She cranked the Prince Henry's engine into life and drove off along Marine Parade, heading for Palm Bay and the home of Effie Dalrymple.

'I really do need to talk to Inspector Page,' she told Effie as soon as she arrived. 'I am sure he will be interested to hear what I have to say about the murder of Mr Grayson.'

'Do you believe he was murdered then?'

'I am sure of it, Effie – and what is more, I believe I know who did it – and, more importantly, why.'

'Do you want to tell me?'

'Not yet, Effie. Not until I have one more piece of evidence; then I shall reveal all. First, though, we need to see the Inspector.'

*

'The Inspector is not here, Mrs Coates,' the desk sergeant said politely. 'Is there anything I can help you with?'

'Only if you can tell me when he will be back.'

'I can't say, madam. He's gone to the Walpole Bay Hotel; that's all I know I'm afraid.'

As they left the police station and crossed the market square, they caught sight of a familiar figure. 'Ratty!' Dorothy called out to him. 'Hold on there for a moment.'

Bumstead stopped and turned. 'How can I 'elp you, missus?' He doffed his cap politely to both of the women.

Dorothy got straight to the point. 'Was that you I saw yesterday down on the promenade? We were there listening to the military band. You were talking with two men.'

Bumstead eyed both women warily. 'Could be, could be.'

The Man at the Walpole Bay Hotel

'Who were they? I only ask because they didn't look local by the way they were dressed. More Romany, or even Irish. They have a certain look about them, the Irish. Very Gaelic in the features of the face. You know, in the way that a Chinaman looks Chinese.'

Bumstead grinned. 'That's true, missus. Though them two was strangers to me.'

'Oh, come along, Ratty, you know everyone around these parts. You must know them, surely?'

'Just a couple of fellas I bumped into when I was 'avin a drink in the Wellington. People wantin' to buy stuff.' He looked knowingly at Dorothy as he said it, and winked. 'That's all. Now I 'ave to be gettin along. Good day, ladies.' With that he doffed his cap once more and made off without saying anything further.

'*Well*, that wasn't very helpful,' Effie huffed as they continued on their way.

'On the contrary, Effie, if you know how Ratty operates, then it was very helpful. You notice he did not contradict me when I suggested the other two might be Irish?'

'How does that help? I don't understand.'

'Fenians, Effie. I'm seeing more Fenians. Now, I think we should go to the Walpole Bay and track down our elusive inspector.'

*

In front of the Walpole Bay Hotel the sight that greeted them was unusual. 'A Black Maria,' Effie said. 'What's that doing here?' The back door of

The Man at the Walpole Bay Hotel

the police van had been banged shut and a constable was locking it. Then the object of their visit walked down the steps.

'Inspector,' Dorothy called, 'a word with you if I might.'

Page brushed the request aside. 'Not now, ladies. Police business calls. Another time.' He swept past them and walked directly to where his own car and driver waited for him.

'Dear me,' Effie said brusquely, 'that inspector really is the most irritating man it has been my displeasure to come across.'

Dorothy smiled. 'Never mind. Let's go in and see if we can find out who has been arrested.'

In the lobby they immediately bumped into Lucinda, her face as forlorn as a wet Monday morning. From the redness of her eyes it was clear she had been crying.

'Whatever is the matter, Lucy dear?'

'Oh, Aunt Dorothy. That policeman, he's arrested Harry. He says he's got evidence that Harry murdered that poor Mr Grayson.' With that Lucinda collapsed into a torrent of tears.

Dorothy rolled her eyes to the ceiling. 'Ouff,' she groaned. '*Stupid* man. He really *does* need setting right. Effie, you stay here and comfort Lucy.'

'What will you do?'

'Go to the police station and sort out Inspector Page, of course,'

*

The Man at the Walpole Bay Hotel

'The Inspector is busy, Mrs Coates,' the sergeant insisted.

'Well, he'll just have to unbusy himself, Sergeant. I insist on seeing him – before he makes a complete ass of himself.'

'I'm very short of time Mrs Coates. I have a suspected murderer in custody and need to interrogate him. Now what is it you want?'

'You have arrested the wrong man, Inspector.'

'I'll be the judge of that, madam. He fits the description of the man the waiter saw in the Fayreness Hotel leaving with Mr Grayson that night. I have the *right* man, Mrs Coates.'

'I have evidence that you are wrong, Inspector. Would you like to hear it?'

'Not at the moment. Now if you don't mind, madam, I have an interview to conduct.'

'It needs to be heard, Inspector.'

'You can tell it to the judge, Mrs Coates. Now *good day.*'

The sergeant nodded his head in sheepish apology to her as Page turned, without waiting for further conversation, and headed back to the accused.

Back in the street Dorothy Coates was shaking her head and was more than a little exasperated. Then she saw something that took her mind away from Page and the arrest. It was the two men she had seen Ratty talking to; the same two Lucinda had pointed out as being in the British Museum Library. It seemed like a good idea to follow them.

The Man at the Walpole Bay Hotel

The men set off in the direction of Westbrook, walking at an easy pace, busy in conversation, and not once looking back in her direction.

Coming near to the railway station they crossed the promenade to where there was a large pavilion, with benches that looked out over the sea. When they reached it they were joined by another man, wearing a seafarer's cap and naval jacket. The three sat down together on one of the benches. The pavilion was open on two sides. The front looked towards the beach and the sea, while on the back those taking their ease viewed the formal gardens and, in the distance, the railway station.

The promenade was busy and Dorothy used the crowd to cover her presence as she took a place on one of the benches just behind the trio. Sitting looking towards the station she was perfectly positioned, back-to-back with the men, and with nothing more than a fretted screen separating her from their conversation. They spoke in low tones and it was difficult to hear all of what was said above the chatter of the passing crowds and the squealing of the gulls overhead; but she heard enough to raise her interest and confirm her suspicions. As the town clock chimed the quarter hour, the three got up and parted. The man in the seafarer's cap headed east along the promenade. Dorothy decided that he was the one to follow.

The man walked briskly and, in her long dress, she found it difficult to keep up with him. Luck helped out when at one point he stopped to fill and light a pipe. When he came to the harbour he turned left and walked along the harbour arm

The Man at the Walpole Bay Hotel

towards the point where the lighthouse marked the end. Dorothy stopped, staying back on the promenade where she took up a casual position, leaning on the railings like a tourist, taking in the view and blending with others doing the same.

From her vantage point she watched as the man stopped at a place where an iron ladder descended the harbour wall. At the bottom there was a dinghy tethered to a ring. He climbed down the ladder and dropped into the small boat. Unshipping the oars, he shoved off and rowed along the harbour wall until he disappeared around the end, under the lee of the lighthouse. She waited until the dinghy had gone from her view then quickly made her way round to the other side of the harbour arm, where the pier led to the steamer jetty. She walked to the end of the pier until she reached the head, paid the one penny entry price and went directly to the viewing platform. There, for a further tuppence pushed into the slot of a telescope, she could watch the progress of the man in the dinghy.

'Right,' she said determinedly under her breath, after the dinghy had finally disappeared into the offing. 'Now let us deal with that *irritating* Inspector Page.'

*

At the police station she marched up to the enquiries desk and confronted the sergeant. 'I wish to see the Inspector – and no excuse will be acceptable. I need to see him *now*.'

The Man at the Walpole Bay Hotel

The sergeant, knowing that she had been brushed away before, was contrite. 'Of course, madam. I'll let him know you are here.'

A constable who had been shuffling papers in the background, sniggered up his sleeve. It wasn't every day that he saw the sergeant given his marching orders by a member of the public. Least of all by a woman. Better still, she looked like she was fit to give the Inspector a rough ride. Page was not popular with the lads in the Muster room. He treated them as if they were incompetent. They referred to him as Cocky Page and hoped he would soon be gone, back to Dover where he came from.

A few minutes later the sergeant was back. He shot a grinning look at the constable. 'Right lad, take this lady to the Inspector's office.' The sergeant, in common with the constables, was not a fan of Page. He also saw him as an interloper and noisy about his own reputation for success in detection.

The constable led the way along a short dingy corridor, past the four cells. She noted that the doors on all of them were open and there were no inmates. That left her wondering what had happened to Donovan and for a moment she supposed he must be in with Page, being interviewed.

'Hello, Mrs Coates,' Page stood up and smiled affably. 'Sorry to be so offhand earlier. Pressure of the job, you understand. Now what can we do for you?'

'Well, for a start, Inspector, you can release Mr Donovan. He is not your murderer. You have the wrong man.'

Page held up a hand, for all the world as if he were in the middle of the road commanding the traffic to stop. 'He has already left, Mrs Coates. Bailed. Earlier this afternoon. A man came into the station and offered to stand surety. We went straight upstairs to the magistrates and it was done right away.'

Dorothy paused, taken aback for a moment. 'Well, that's a start. Now, let me tell you how I believe poor Mr Grayson met his untimely end.'

Before she could say more, the DC poked his head round the door. 'Excuse me, sir. Need a word. Just got news in on the missing German gent. Seems he was likely acquainted with our suspect.'

Page stood up. 'Beg pardon, Mrs Coates, we shall have to finish our talk another time.' He took Dorothy by the arm and guided her out of his office. 'Wait for me, Constable; won't be a minute.'

Page left Dorothy at the enquiries desk and went back to his office.

She stood there for a moment, then a thought occurred to her. 'Sergeant,' she said. 'Do you have a record of the person who stood surety for Mr Donovan?'

The sergeant reached down under the counter and pulled up a heavy ledger. He opened it and ran a finger down the page of the day's record. 'Yes, madam, I do. It was a gentleman by the name of

Trevelyan. Mr Seymour Trevelyan. Proper posh he was too.'

'Well, now,' Dorothy nodded, 'that *is* very interesting.'

*

It was late afternoon when Dorothy drew the Prince Henry to a halt at the kerb outside the Walpole Bay Hotel. Inside she found Effie and Lucinda, sitting in the bar, together with Harry Donovan. Lucinda and Harry were holding hands in a very intimate fashion.

'Dorothy,' Effie said on seeing her friend. 'We're having a cocktail to celebrate Harry's return. Will you have a Negroni?'

'You know, I think I will. It has been a very productive day; I'm feeling quite pooped. I shall tell you about it later, Effie – over dinner. Lucy dear, will you join us? You too, Harry.'

'That is very kind of you, Mrs Coates,' Harry said, 'but I rather thought I would take Lucy out to dinner myself. If you don't object, that is?'

'Of course, of course. You do not need my approval. Lucy is a grown-up girl. Effie, we should pop off and have a quiet talk somewhere. I have a few interesting things to tell you. Come along. I'll drive you home and we can talk as we go.'

'We have a rendezvous,' Dorothy said when they reached Effie's house. 'Quite a late one.'

'Oh, that's nice. Who are we meeting?'

The Man at the Walpole Bay Hotel

'Well, we're not actually meeting. More observing.'

Effie looked puzzled. 'Do tell.'

'I followed those two bad characters this afternoon. You know, the two Lucy recognised.'

'The ones you thought were Fenians?'

'Precisely so – and they are. I am now certain of it. I overheard them talking with another man. They are hatching some kind of plot. I think they may be planning to bring contraband ashore. I'm certain there is a ship waiting out there, just over the horizon; with an illegal cargo.'

'Brandy?'

'No, Effie, guns. I think they are gunrunners.'

'Oh, my goodness. For the Irish cause?'

'For the Irish cause. We need to keep a watch at Botany Bay. On that big cave. That is where they are planning to come ashore; I heard that much of their conversation. We need to observe them, and then alert the authorities.'

'Might that not be a bit dangerous?'

'Yes, but we shall keep our distance. I suggest we install ourselves in the old flint folly, up on the cliff. From the top of the walls one gets a clear view of the beach and the cave.'

'When does this all happen?'

'I don't know, but after dark, so we should go to the Fayreness Hotel, have our dinner there, then when the light has gone we can go from there to the folly.'

By ten o'clock it was dark. The two women made their way along the clifftop path till they arrived at the old folly. They walked around the walls to the entrance, which was no more than a gaping breach in the flintwork. 'Hold on a minute,' Dorothy said, and switched on a torch. 'It's pretty overgrown in here, so be careful.'

Inside, the folly was a simple rotunda with window openings; just rectangular gaps without frames or fittings, but they afforded a good clear view down to the beach.

'Right, nothing to do now but wait.' Dorothy shuffled herself into a comfortable position and prepared to sit it out.

Just before midnight they saw some activity down on the beach. A half-moon shed enough light to make out the motion of a small boat coming ashore. The two women shuffled closer to the window opening. They were so intent on watching, they did not at first notice the moving shadows that were approaching the folly. The shadows moved closer.

'Oh, my God,' Dorothy hissed. 'Visitors.'

A moment later three figures entered through the door opening. 'What have we here, lads? Snoopers, I'd say.' The accent was a strong Irish brogue and the face of the speaker was clearly the seafaring man Dorothy had seen earlier in the day.

'Best do for them, Shaun,' one of the others said. The seafarer pulled a knife from his coat. 'Make it quick,' another voice called.

Dorothy froze. The seafarer came closer. As he put out a hand to grab her and one of the others started to move towards Effie, there was the sharp bark of a gunshot. The seafarer shouted in pain and cursed loudly. There was a second shot.

'Holy mother of God, get out!' one of them shouted. All three assailants scrambled to get through the door and away. There was the sound of a hurried retreat and then nothing; just quiet, and stillness. Dorothy turned to look at Effie.

'Are you all right? What the *devil* was that?' It was then she saw the gun Effie was holding. *'Good grief, Effie. What on earth are you doing with that?'*

'Max's old service pistol,' Effie said calmly. 'Broom-handle Mauser; 9 millimetre. And you did say it might be dangerous tonight – so I thought why not. I used to be a crack shot on the range when we were in Berlin, you know.'

They waited for a while until they were sure the others had gone, then went to the cliff edge from where they could see more of the beach. There was nothing – it was deserted.

Chapter 11

More clues

It was early morning and fresh as Inspector Page came down to the dining room of the Seagull Guest House, where he was lodging while he worked on the Grayson case.

The landlady had lavished a good English breakfast on him, with the insistence that it would set him up for the day. Unfortunately, the breakfast had come together with interruptions; punctuated by her endless opinions.

'I can't be doing with these foreigners,' she insisted. 'They have a very poor breakfast. All that bread and fancy pastry stuff. That's no way to start a day. A man needs a good filling for a good day's work. Kippers, bacon, eggs, porridge, sausages. That's what I say. No wonder them Frenchies can't win a war. Look at that Napoleon fella. Sent his lot off to fight with nothing but a stick of bread down their trousers. That's no good.'

The Man at the Walpole Bay Hotel

Page was not really listening; his mind was on the case. He buttered a slice of toast. 'If you say so, Mrs Clacket.'

'I do, Inspector Page, I do ... and they took a fair walloping from them Prussians not fifty years back. Didn't they?'

Page just nodded, and bit into his toast. 'Nice marmalade,' he managed to mumble.

'Homemade is best, Inspector. More tea?' Page agreed, in the hopes of being left to get on with his thoughts. Mrs Clacket, however, showed no signs of giving up.

'Of course, them Germans are like us. Meat is what a man needs for his breakfast. They eat a lot of sausages, you know. Partial to a good sausage I am.' She thought about that for a moment, then added, 'Mind you, some of the stuff they eat is a bit funny – they eat a lot of pickled cabbage, I heard, but they cook it. Now that's a bit strange wouldn't you say. And them sausages of theirs – well, they're not proper sausages, are they? Not like what we 'ave – you know – proper. I like a proper British banger m'self. Still, them German ones is meat – and that's what makes the difference. I can see them Boche walking all over the Frenchies again – and us having to bail 'em out.

'That Kaiser Bill's men are tricky as well you know. I heard they was over here already, spying out the land, like. Trying to find out our secrets. And there's another thing I wouldn't mind putting a half a crown on. I'd bet my Sunday drawers on one of them being who did for that Mr Grayson

The Man at the Walpole Bay Hotel

gentlemen. Him what went over the cliff top at Botany Bay.'

Page hurriedly finished his toast and washed it down with a gulp of tea. Pulling the napkin from where it was tucked into his collar, he got up and made his excuses for a rapid departure. He nodded to a couple of men sitting at another table as he passed them. 'Good morning, gentlemen,' he said.

'And the top of the morning to you, sir,' one of them replied in a strong Dublin accent.

The morning air was still fresh for August, as Page walked briskly down to the town. It was good to be away from Mrs Clacket's prattling, and with his mind clear he began to turn the case over in his head. He was entering the market square when something the landlady had said rang a bell. German spies, she had said. Well what if Grayson had spotted something suspicious, uncovered a spy ring, and *they* had eliminated him. Now that might explain why he had been pushed off the top. Hadn't the waiter reported he'd often seen Grayson out walking the cliffs, with binoculars. Keen birdwatcher, he'd said – and also interested in the ships that came and moored out in the roads of Margate harbour, waiting to carry their cargoes up to the London docks and unload at the riverside warehouses. Perhaps Mrs Clacket was right. Perhaps German agents had done for him. The more he thought about it the more it seemed credible.

'Right, Constable Godley,' Page said as he entered the office. 'What have you got for me this morning?'

The DC flipped over the pages of his notebook. 'Grayson had made a will. It was drawn up some time ago by local solicitors, Goldsmith and Pratt. There were bequests, sir, but no mention of Donovan, so I think we can rule that one out. Scotland Yard came up with something interesting, though. It seems that the missing German – the one in the papers, Herr Weber – well, he may be connected with what we have going on down here in Margate. It appears he is an associate of Donovan.'

'Is he now?'

'Yes, sir. Donovan's cleaning lady came forward when she saw Weber in the newspaper. According to her, Weber had visited Donovan several times in his Kensington abode. Sometimes he'd stayed there overnight.'

Page ran a finger over his top lip. 'Did he by Jove.'

'There's more, sir. A woman at the British Museum Library, one of the librarians, has identified Weber as a man she saw acting strangely there last week.'

'Strangely, you say. What was he doing?'

'He pulled out a lot of books and turned over the pages quickly, without really looking at them. She said he didn't seem to be rightly interested in the books. He just kept shuffling them around. She says, at the same time he kept looking about him; sort of nervous, like he was watching out for someone. She didn't think much of it at the time apparently. It was only when she saw his picture in the papers that she thought she ought to report it.'

Page was nodding sagely. 'I wonder; maybe Mrs Clacket had something there.'

'Who's Mrs Clacket, sir?'

'Oh, just the landlady at the lodgings where I'm staying. She has theories about spies – along with other things – like sausages. Seems half the ladies in Margate are sleuths, Godley. But in this case, she might just have hit on something.'

'Sir?'

'What if our German was a spy? And what if our Mr Donovan was maybe his contact here in England? They could have been using a book code. Weber could have marked one of those books. That's how it's done, you know.'

'Or he could just have left something in one of them, sir. What I understand is called a dead letter box.'

'Yes, that's a possibility. The German leaves it there; Donovan collects it later.'

DC Godley furrowed his brow. 'But where does Benedict Grayson come into this? Do we think he was a spy, too?'

'No, not in my book. Consider the scene, Godley. Donavan has the information. He has to pass it on. How does he do that?'

'Take a boat to Germany – or maybe Holland. Margate is close enough to either.'

'Yes, or meet someone on the beach and hand it over. A small boat then takes it to one of the bigger ships out there offshore.'

'And Grayson sees them.'

'Exactly. So they push him over the cliff.'

Godley took to nodding his head vigorously. 'I think you might have solved it, sir.'

'Possibly, but that's only a theory, Constable. Now we have to prove it.'

*

Donovan was sitting at a café table on the promenade. After a while a man in a bowler hat came and sat down beside him.

'Seymour, have you seen this?' Donovan smacked down noisily on the table with a tightly folded newspaper he'd been reading.

Trevelyan languidly picked up the paper and spread it out on the table. 'I don't know, dear boy – have I?'

Donovan prodded the front page with a finger. 'They found Ernst – at Gravesend – lying face down and bloated on the foreshore.'

'Yes, I know.'

'Well, what are we going to do?'

Trevelyan cocked his head to one side and raised his eyebrows. 'Do? Why, we do nothing of course.'

'I thought you were going to arrange to dispose of the body?'

The Man at the Walpole Bay Hotel

'And so we did. We floated poor Ernst on his farewell journey. Bobbing down the Thames on the ebbing tide.'

'Well, they found him.'

'Of course. That is what we wanted.'

'There's bound to be an enquiry.'

'Exactly, dear boy, and it will conclude that he committed suicide. You see, we took the precaution of tying a bit of old rope round his neck and pulling it up tight before we launched him on his final journey. It rather conveniently covered the incision in his carotid artery where he was stabbed. We previously arranged for the rope to be roughly parted under strain. The coroner will conclude he tried to hang himself off the bridge at Blackfriars. The rope was rotten and Ernst fell, without ceremony, into the filthy waters of the Thames.'

'Why would they think Blackfriars?'

'We left the other end of the rope neatly tied to the Blackfriars bridge parapet. It has been organised for a member of the public to find it. They will report it to the peelers; ergo, conclusion of case. No further investigation. Whereas, if we had buried him in the woods, the investigation would be ongoing. There is nothing quite like producing the body to satisfy those simple souls at the constabulary. Now, how are you getting on with that girl. Have you managed to get the second book from her. It may have clues, Harry. Clues to where the papers have gone.'

'It's proving difficult.'

The Man at the Walpole Bay Hotel

Trevelyan stood up. 'Well, woo her, Harry, woo her. I know you are good at that sort of thing.'

*

Dorothy picked up the telephone earpiece and held it to her ear. With her free hand she tapped on the cradle bar.

'What number, please?' a woman at the telephone exchange asked politely.

'Margate 213,' Dorothy said, then waited.

'Putting you through, madam,' the operator replied. Some clicking and whirring followed, then the sound of the ringing tone. After a few rings, a voice responded, 'Margate 213, Dalrymple residence.'

'Freida, it's Mrs Coates. Is your mistress at home?'

'Yes, madam, I will call her right away.'

Dorothy waited. After half a minute she heard the tap, tap, tap of approaching footsteps on the hall parquet, then, 'Dorothy, how are you?'

'I'm perfectly well, thank you, Effie. Now, I've been having thoughts about those men up at the folly, and particularly that seagoing fellow, the one you let have it in the arm. Good shot that, by the way.'

'I tried to make it a flesh wound, you know. I didn't really want to break his arm bone, poor man.'

'*Poor man*! Humbug, Effie dear. You heard what they said. They were going to *do* for us. The *very* idea of it. He got no more than he justly deserved. Now, enough of that, I have a small errand for you – if you will.'

'Of course, I should be delighted. What is it you would like me to do?'

'As I was saying – about that seagoing fellow. As you know, I watched him row away in a dinghy. Well, it suddenly occurred to me, there was a name on the back of it. So, it could be the tender to a larger boat. I mean, he must have been rowing to somewhere, and it would be too far to go to Holland in that little cockleshell. No, there must be a bigger boat out there; just below the horizon, I should think.'

'So, what would you like me to do?'

'The name on that boat was *Gelderland*. Now, if it's anchored out there in the estuary, the harbour master should know about it, and have a record of its flag and its owners. I would like you to go to the harbour office and make enquiries. I would do it, but I need to track down Ratty. I have a question or two for him.'

*

Dorothy was not sure where she might find Bumstead at that time of the day. It was not yet ten o'clock; too early for him to be drinking. Ratty was a man who liked his pint, but he was also meticulously circumspect about his hours. He would not take a drink before luncheon.

However, there were opportunities to be found in the licensed establishments. Dealings of a more

The Man at the Walpole Bay Hotel

discreet nature, conducted under counters and in quiet corners. The sorts of transaction that had put more than a crust or two on Ratty's table. So she could not rule out finding him in one of those places at this hour trying to broker some kind of deal. Therefore, a morning trawl of the public houses and hotels in the area might be the answer.

She started out with a walk into the town, beginning on the outskirts with a quick call into the Nayland Rock Hotel, and then the Shakespeare public house. Neither had seen him for some time, but there was no shortage of venues to investigate. She moved on to the Kings Head in the High Street, then to the Cottage, the Brewers Arms and the Phoenix. Close to Market Place she tried the Queens Head, then the Wellington Hotel, followed by the George Hotel. But Ratty was being elusive.

By eleven o'clock she had visited all 28 establishments in the centre and went back to her house. There she climbed into the Prince Henry and drove up Fort Hill. Her first stop was the Brewery Tap; not there. Then the Fountain; hadn't seen him for a week or more. It was the same story in the Hoy Arms, the Prospect and the Clifton Arms. No one had seen Ratty for days. It began to look like he'd taken the pledge; given up the demon drink.

In the Ethelbert Hotel she struck her first piece of luck. 'He was in here this morning,' the landlord tersely informed her. 'Him and that tatty old lurcher of his. Said he was going to walk the thing up on the cliffs; over by Palm Bay.'

Dorothy knew she had found Ratty the minute she saw the motorcar. It was the only Rolls Royce in Margate. The long snout with the flying lady mascot on the end of its nose was unmistakable.

She saw him in the distance as she brought the Prince Henry to a halt; a figure on the skyline. She waved but he didn't seem to notice so she gave two long blasts on the Prince Henry's klaxon. Ratty stopped, looked in her direction and, when she waved again, began walking towards her.

'Allo, missus,' Ratty said as he reached her. 'Nice day. Old Toby likes a walk up 'ere. Sniffs around the bushes. Likes to cock 'is leg on the council benches. No respecter of authority that dog. Won't listen to a word from me. Just does what 'ee wants.'

'A bit like his master then, Ratty.'

'Now that ain't nice, missus.'

Dorothy smiled. 'True enough though. Which brings me to the reason for seeking you out this morning. When I saw you the other day outside the Wellington with those two men you gave me the wink. I know that wink, Ratty. It usually means you have something up your sleeve.'

'Do it?'

'You've been keeping bad company, Ratty. Those two men you were with at the Wellington – the Irishmen; Fenians, are they?'

Ratty Bumstead said nothing, but the wry look on his face was enough to confirm what she had guessed.

'What are you up to with them?'

The Man at the Walpole Bay Hotel

'Just business, missus.' Bumstead's face snatched a quick smirk.

'Are you selling them guns? I do hope not. That would be unpatriotic, and *very* illegal, Ratty.' He didn't reply, but instead reached into his pocket and took out a tobacco pouch.

'Well?'

Bumstead ignored the question. He produced a pocket knife, pulled the blade open and cut a thick slice from a gluey plug of tobacco, which he stuffed into his mouth. He slowly closed the knife again, and put the pouch back into his pocket, all the while chewing on the tobacco. He spat a blob of brown goo onto the ground. 'Cor bless you, I ain't selling guns, missus.' A good-humoured smile came back onto his face.

'You have done, though.'

'True, but not to the boyos from over in Dublin. I do all my business a long way from 'ome. Africa. Never make a mess on yer own doorstep – that's my motto.'

'So what's your business with the Fenians, Ratty? Come clean.'

He spat out another thick glob of tobacco juice, sending it splattering on the pavement. He leant close and she could smell the cloying odour of the rum-soaked tobacco on his breath. 'I'm not *selling* guns, missus,' he hissed quietly in her ear, 'I'm buying.' He stepped back from Dorothy and resumed a normal voice. 'Not from them, of course; from their source. They give me an introduction; I give them a little sweetener. It's business, missus. Just business.'

The Man at the Walpole Bay Hotel

'That's immoral, Ratty.'

'That's the way of the world, missus. Now, if you want immoral, you just take a gander at that lot in London, sittin in their palace. Not a straight'n among 'em.'

'Who, *the King*!' Dorothy protested in a voice of indignance.

'Luv a duck, no. That lot of politicians in the Palace of Westminster. So crooked there's not one of them could lie down straight in 'is bed. You look to them if you wants to criticise. My business is honest. I buys and I sells. Fair prices all round. Nuffin to do wiv me if that load of Johnny foreigners in Africa want to go abaht shootin each uvver. We're soon gonna be doin plenty of that up 'ere, the way things is goin, missus. You mark my words.'

*

'Over here,' Effie called, and waved to Dorothy as she climbed the steps at the Walpole Bay Hotel. 'Come and have a seat on the veranda; I have some interesting news.'

Dorothy took off a large straw sunhat and placed it on a table, then flopped down into a softly upholstered armchair next to her friend. She let out a deep sigh. 'It's been a gloriously warm day and I'm parched. What do you say to a couple of iced Pimm's?'

Effie smiled at that. 'I'd say it was a very splendid idea. Look, there's Simpson. Why don't

The Man at the Walpole Bay Hotel

we ask him. I'm sure he'll have a word with the barman and marshal a waiter to our cause.'

Dorothy raised an arm and flapped a hand at the concierge, who immediately came over to them. 'Simpson, would you be so awfully kind as to arrange two nicely chilled Pimm's for me and Mrs Dalrymple here?'

Simpson gave a deferential nod. 'Of course, ladies. With borage or mint?'

'Oh borage; one should always use borage. Mint only in *extremis*.'

'And cucumber,' Effie added quickly. 'A very thin slice if you please.'

'Very good, ladies.

'And I think without the orange and strawberries,' Dorothy added. 'We don't want to make a fruit salad out of the thing. It is the latest fad you know, Effie. I believe certain types even add pineapple.'

She waited until Simpson was out of earshot then said, 'Do tell me what you have discovered.'

Effie leant forward across the low table that sat between them. 'The *Gelderland*,' she said in not much above a whisper, 'is flying a Panamanian flag of convenience, but it's real home is Hamburg. Its registered owner is Nordhausen Handel GmbH.'

'German.'

'Exactly, my dear – and there's more. The chairman of the company is one Rudolf Schneider. I took steps to make a telephone call to an old friend of mine at the Foreign Office. It would appear that Herr Schneider has a private steam yacht. Or perhaps I should say, he *had* a yacht. With the declaration of hostilities it was hurriedly transferred to a small company – in Belfast.'

'Was it now? Well, I never. Does this yacht have a name?'

'*Regina Maris*.'

'Well done.'

'There is more. I made a call to Lloyds. I have a broker in one of the syndicates, you know. He checked on the shipping register, and what do you think? The *Regina Maris* was recently moved to a berth in Bristol.'

'Effie, you *have* been busy.'

'Yes, but I'm not sure this bears on poor Mr Grayson's death. Does it?'

Dorothy looked thoughtful. 'I really don't know. We have lots of pieces to the puzzle. I'm just not sure if we have them all and, if we do, how they fit together. Though it *is* peculiar, do you not think, that these threads always lead back to Ireland – ah, here are the Pimm's. Precisely what is needed to revitalise the thought processes.'

Effie lifted her glass. 'Cheerio and down the hatch, old thing. Oh, and bye the bye, how is it going along between Lucy and her young man?'

'I'd say there was definitely romance in the air.'

'How exciting. Do we think his intentions are honourable? He is a very handsome young man, and that can be dangerous, you know.'

'I'm sure he is – but look, here *is* Lucy. You can ask her yourself.'

Dorothy stood up. 'Lucy dear,' she called out. 'Over here. Come and join us.'

The Man at the Walpole Bay Hotel

'Yes, do sit down with us,' Effie invited. 'We're having Pimm's, and puzzling over the dilemma of Mr Grayson; would you like one?'

Lucinda greeted the idea with enthusiasm. 'Sounds spiffing. Have you concluded anything on Mr Grayson's death, Aunt?'

'Not really. The more I find out, the less clear the whole thing becomes. It really is a maze. I hope you had a nice time the other evening when you went out to supper. How is Harry, by the way?'

'Yes, do tell,' Effie pleaded. 'Is there romance in the air?'

Lucinda offered a coy smile. 'You'll have to wait and see, Effie. He is by far the nicest and most attentive man I have ever met ...,' Lucinda hesitated, '... though, he has moments of distraction. Especially with that over-diligent policeman, Inspector Page. Did you read about the German found dead on the river bank at Gravesend?'

Dorothy indicated she had.

'Page has been pestering Harry about that, too.'

'Oh?'

'They are saying Harry knew the man.'

'Are they suggesting foul play? Surely not.'

Lucinda shook her head vigorously. 'He has a cast-iron alibi. He was in Margate at the time. And anyway the coroner's verdict was suicide. The German hung himself off Blackfriars Bridge. No, the real question is, was this German a spy. That would put Harry in an awkward spot, poor darling.'

The Man at the Walpole Bay Hotel

'Ah, reinforcements,' Effie said, pointing to an approaching waiter. 'Here comes Herbert with your Pimm's. Take a good big nip of that. That'll buck you up.'

'While I remember,' Lucinda said, 'I'm not sure if this has any bearing on anything.' She dived into her handbag and pulled out a letter. 'My friend, Amelia Blain, wrote to me. She works at the Library.' Lucinda passed it over to Dorothy. 'The interesting bit starts at the bottom of the page. Do read it and tell me what you think.' Lucinda pointed a finger at the passage ...

... I thought you might like to know, there was another peculiar incident here in the Library today. Two men came to my desk and asked which was the section for Ornithology. I did not consider it out of the ordinary at first, but when I passed that aisle on another errand I noticed something strange. They were taking out the books from the shelves, shaking the pages open, then putting them back. When they had gone along the entire section they simply left. I had not seen these men before, though their actions did put me very much in mind of those two who came in on a previous occasion. The two rough-looking types who ran off after that German man. The one who did that dreadful act of suicide. I am not sure if they are in any manner connected but I have been asked to give a description to

the constables because, of course, I had already identified the photograph of the German when he visited here. The world really does seem to have gone mad ...

'What did you think of what was in the letter?' Effie asked after Lucinda had left them. 'Does it help?'

'No, Effie, I don't think it does. It just adds to the confusion. Why don't we ask Simpson for a sheet of paper and a pencil. Then we can set out a scrabble of what we know – and we should order two more Pimm's. This detection business is thirsty work.'

Simpson placed a blank sheet of quarto on the table. 'There we are, ladies. Is there anything else you require?'

'Oh, yes please, Simpson, could you refresh the Pimm's, do you think?' Effie said taking charge of the sheet of paper. 'If you dictate, Dorothy, I shall record.'

Dorothy rubbed a finger across her forehead and narrowed her eyes in concentration. 'Very good, what do we know?'

'One: Mr Grayson is dead.'

'Two: Inspector Page has conclude he was murdered.'

'Three: the German, Herr Weber is also dead. So, two murders.'

'But ... ,' Effie jabbed the air with her pencil, '... there is no motive for Mr Grayson, and the German was said to be suicide.'

The Man at the Walpole Bay Hotel

'True, though they could still be murders,' Dorothy offered. 'We just don't know. Better note that down. What next? Yes, there are Fenians in the town; two at least, and we know their names, courtesy of Ratty – he told me the other day: Thomas Burn, and Daniel O'Connell. We know they are gun runners, Ratty gave us the lowdown on that too.'

'You know, Dorothy. He has been most useful, that Ratty. Come back all I said about him in the past,'

'Precisely. Now, where was I?'

'Fenians,' Effie reminded her.

'Ah yes, the Fenians had a rendezvous with an Irish American, one Jackson Molloy of Boston. We know that because the clerk at the office of the paddlers told us so.'

'Do we know he *is* Irish, though?'

'I think we can be fairly certain of that, Effie – but put a point interrogative against that entry.'

'Done.'

'To continue. We overheard one of the Fenians saying to the American something about the wrong person having been got, which in their parlance could translate as killed – but we don't know to which one that relates – or if indeed it relates to either. It could have been a reference to something else altogether. So, please mark down another interrogative against that, Effie.'

'We did find that American cigarette packet, Dorothy. Up on the cliff not far from where poor Mr Grayson went over. There can't be many Americans in the area – would you think?'

'Good point, Effie, and although it was found a good fifty yards further along the clifftop, we also know the wind was in that direction so it was most likely dropped back where Mr Grayson went over.

Now we come to the *Gelderland* and the seafarer, the one you shot.'

That gave Effie pause for thought. 'Do you think we should tell Inspector Page about that? I suppose it ought to be reported.'

Dorothy pursed her lips, a serious expression spread across her face. 'Could be a two-edged sword, that one. Page might take a dim view of you shooting that man.'

'Self-defence,' Effie protested.

'I take it you do have a licence for that Mauser gun of yours – do you?'

Effie looked a trifle sheepish. She shook her head. 'Not really. It was in the baggage when we came back to England. When Max passed away, God bless him, I was going to throw it into the sea. But, you know how it is, it had sentimental value – so I kept it.'

'Well, as it turned out it's just as well you did, or we should both be basking in the glory of the hereafter by now. Right, back to the seafarer.' Dorothy rolled her eyes up to the ceiling. 'He connects the Fenians to the *Gelderland*. The *Gelderland* is actually German, as we know, and that brings us round to the document in Lucy's bird book: a set of minutes for a meeting. It is very plain to see where this all leads us. The Germans were approached by some Irish Americans at their

The Man at the Walpole Bay Hotel

Washington embassy and, at a meeting there, agreed to provide assistance to the Irish cause.'

Effie put down the pencil. 'That all seems to make perfect sense – but does it really bring us any closer to who did for Mr Grayson – and why?'

Dorothy was about to answer when she spotted Simpson approaching. 'Oh, good, here's the Pimm's. I thought perhaps you'd forgotten us, Simpson.'

The concierge smiled. 'Perish the thought, dear ladies.'

He turned to leave but Dorothy called after him. 'Simpson, one more thing.'

'Mrs Coates?'

'You knew the recently departed Mr Grayson.'

'I did, he patronised the Walpole from time to time. Was there a question?'

'Would you say he was a regular type? Not mixed up with unsavoury sorts, or given perhaps to acts which might in their failure drive him to take his own life?'

Simpson reacted with mild surprise. 'Oh no, Mrs Coates. He was a pillar of respectability. I can vouch for that. I would stake my life upon it.'

'Well, that won't be necessary, Simpson, but thank you nonetheless.'

'That only leaves us with one other thing,' Dorothy said, after taking a sip of her drink. 'Harry. I do not believe he is all he seems, or pretends to be.'

The Man at the Walpole Bay Hotel

'Hmm, I have similar feelings, Dorothy. A personable young man – but is he just a little too personable.'

'Indeed. There are questions. What was his relationship with Herr Weber? And why is he posing as a watcher of birds, when he clearly knows little of the subject?'

Effie frowned. 'I also get the feeling he has more than just a romantic interest in Lucy. You notice how he was in her room when she discovered the break-in, and he shows more than a passing interest in her books.'

'And, Effie, there is a thread of connection through Lucy, and the library, to the Fenians.'

Effie nodded sagely. 'That young man is not all he seems.'

'And there is yet another thing,' Dorothy said, a note of uncertainty hanging on the words. 'Seymour Trevelyan, the signatory of the surety for Harry's release. That name has a familiar ring. I can't quite place it, but I am sure I've heard it before.'

*

Inspector Page had read the headline over his breakfast in the Seagull Guest House. He was still coming to terms with it as he arrived at the police station. 'Retreat! Retreat! Who'd have thought it,' he said to the desk sergeant. His words carried a note of disbelief. 'The Boche have only gone and kicked us out of Mons. The British Army *never* retreats.'

The Man at the Walpole Bay Hotel

'A black day indeed, Inspector,' the sergeant replied. 'This came in earlier in the morning.' He handed Page a single sheet. 'Circulated to all stations, sir. Seems we have to be on the lookout for spies. It says here that German agents are suspected of operating in southern coastal regions; especially Essex, Kent and Sussex.'

Page ran his eyes across the sheet. 'Thank you, Sergeant. Where's DC Godley? Is he around?'

'Muster room most likely, sir.'

Page walked smartly down the corridor and stuck his head round the muster room door. 'Godley. In my office – in five minutes.'

DC Godley, who was drinking tea, and talking about football with two uniformed constables, immediately put his cup down. 'Right away, Inspector.'

'The whole world's going to the dogs, lad,' Page said as DC Godley stepped into the office. 'As if a military defeat's not bad enough – now there is news that we've got secret agents at work, right here on our doorstep. In Margate no less.' Page moved the paper across the desk.

Godley read it. 'Do we think this has anything to do with the Grayson case, sir?'

'That's *exactly* what we think, lad. It seems the most likely situation, and in my experience if a thing seems likely to be – then it generally is. Trouble, of course, is the magistrates and judges will be asking for something a bit more solid than 'likely'. Let's consider for a moment what we have.'

Godley looked sceptical. 'Not a lot at the moment, sir.'

'We have a dead German.'

'Didn't he commit suicide? How does that help?'

'Might not be suicide. Could have been arranged. A red herring. Anyway, that doesn't make him any less dead – and, more important, he was a known associate of Donovan. Donovan's cleaning lady says the German stayed at his place at least once, so they were close associates.'

'But that doesn't help us with the Grayson murder – does it?'

'I'm still sticking with my theory that Grayson was the innocent bystander. He blundered into something up there on the clifftops and Donovan bumped him off. That's the most likely explanation and, as I said, likely is usually what is.'

'But it's not evidence, sir.'

'No, but we do have the statement of the waiter at the Fayreness. He saw them both together. He also asserts that Donovan was sporting a pair of binoculars. What's a man doing in the night with binoculars? Sounds highly suspicious.'

'Do you think that might be enough of a case, sir? It's still not solid evidence.'

'No, Godley, it isn't. So we must find some. I think we need to put a tail on Mr Donovan. Speak with the sergeant. See if he's got a constable who's any good out of uniform. Let's give friend Donovan some rope – see if he'll oblige by hanging himself.'

'I'll see the sergeant right away, sir.'

'Oh, and while your passing the muster room, see if you can rustle up a cuppa. Tea lubricates the mind, Godley. Stimulates the thought process.'

Chapter 12

Contraband

Trevelyan looked agitated. An unusual state of affairs for a man generally unperturbed by the foibles and peccadillos of the doubtful world he inhabited. 'We need to find that document Harry, and soon. Otherwise it becomes worthless.'

Donavan, unlike Trevelyan, appeared at ease. 'I'm entertaining the young lady this evening. I have to take it slowly or she'll suspect I have other motives.'

'Hmm. Results, Harry. We need results. This damn war is getting ahead of us. What about the guns? Where are they now?'

'Nicely squared away, Seymour. A barn out on the London road. They're to be moved next Friday. Apparently everything is arranged.'

'Which only makes it all the more imperative that we retrieve the document. Its value is fast diminishing.'

The Man at the Walpole Bay Hotel

*

On the stroke of midnight the landlord at the Wellington guided the last of his clientele out into Duke Street, shot the bolts on the doors and closed up the shutters.

Round the corner at the Bulls Head the same thing was being done there. Outside, in the market square, the night air still carried the warmth from what had been a scorching August day. Around the perimeter and along the streets the dull light from the gas lamps splashed the flagstones with circular pools of yellow, each one an isolated island set in a sea of black. Anyone walking at that hour would be obliged to travel in darkness from one haven of light to the next; though there were few about. Most people in the town had long since gone to their beds. Margate was shutting down for the night.

The last customer to leave the Cottage Inn was a man in his early thirties. He left the building and made his way down the High Street. His gait was unsteady; he had been drinking solidly since lunchtime. At the bottom he reached the promenade where he progressed towards the harbour, weaving precariously. A bit before he reached the harbour he turned right into King Street, a narrow, poorly lit thoroughfare, not much wider than an alley and mostly swathed by the dark. At the far end he could see the light of the George Hotel; this became his beacon. Moments after he had entered the street, the shadow of

The Man at the Walpole Bay Hotel

another figure passed through the final pool of lamplight at the entrance, and sank into the same anonymity of darkness. The figure moved quietly in soft canvas shoes.

About halfway along the street, the man stopped. He staggered up to a doorway, leaned against its lintel and fumbled with his clothing. The splash of a steady stream of urine broke the silence. A few yards back, still hidden in the darkness, the second figure stopped. It waited. The stillness returned. Relieved, the drunken man moved on.

When he reached the George Hotel he again stopped; this time he took a packet of cigarettes from his coat and, with a shaking hand, struck a match to light one. In his state of carelessness he dropped the lighted match onto his silk tie and it immediately flamed. He gasped and slapped frantically at it. The exertion was too much for him; he blacked out and fell.

The figure who had been following him stepped quickly out of the blackness to reveal a strongly built man in a grey tweed suit with a bushy moustache. A paperboy cap was pulled hard down onto his head. In a single move he pulled the burning tie clear and threw it to one side. He leaned close and put his ear to the other's mouth, listening for the sound of air. There was the faintest hint of a breath. The man in the tweed suit pressed his hands tightly around the throat of his victim. He squeezed until the breathing stopped and all life had gone. After several minutes he scooped up the limp body and carried it into the hotel yard, where he propped it up against a wall.

The Man at the Walpole Bay Hotel

*

A constable knocked on the door of Page's office. 'Inspector, sir. One of the constables has just reported in. There's another body, sir. Been found out back of the stable yard of the George Hotel.'

The sergeant's face appeared over the shoulder of the constable. 'They've covered the body and I've left another constable standing guard. I've informed the coroner over in Ramsgate. They're sending a Doc to take a look. Once they're done I'll have the cadaver moved to the hospital mortuary. Will you go over to look at it, sir.'

Page made a negative motion with his head. 'No, too busy with the Grayson case. Find Godley, Sergeant. Send him over to take a look – and have we heard anything from that constable we sent out to tail Donovan?'

'No, sir, but he's under instruction to phone in if he discovers anything significant; otherwise he'll make out his report at the end of the day.'

The town clock had just finished striking three when the sergeant poked his head round the door again. 'Constable Bradshaw just reported in, sir. Do you want to see him?'

Page sniffed. 'Why? Who's Constable Bradshaw?'

'The man we sent out to tail Donovan.'

'And?'

'Not a lot really. He followed him over to a couple of public houses, then Donovan gave him the slip.'

'He lost him?'

'I'm afraid he did.'

'Which pubs did he go into?'

Before the sergeant could answer, the phone on Page's desk rang. Page held up a finger to indicate the sergeant should wait. 'Godley.' He looked over to the sergeant, still holding up the finger.

Godley's voice came through, thin and tinny, penetrating the Bakelite earpiece just enough for the wating sergeant to hear. 'I think you need to come over, Inspector. The doctor's all finished up here, but there's something strange. I think you need to see it before it's moved. There are two men with a cart waiting to take the corpse to the mortuary.'

'So, what's so strange, Godley?'

'Well, sir, I'm fairly certain the body is that of Mr Donovan.'

'Oh my word. I'll be right over.'

*

The distance from the police station to the George Hotel was no more than five hundred yards. When Page arrived there, the body was still in the position in which it had been found: propped up against the wall. It had been covered over with a large white linen tablecloth from the hotel restaurant. The hotel manager and the cellarman who had found the body, stood nearby.

The Man at the Walpole Bay Hotel

'I've taken statements,' Godley confided, 'but I've kept these two here in case you want to talk with them. The cellarman found the body first thing this morning, just before six when he was putting out the empty barrels for collection.' Godley pulled back the tablecloth. 'Face is badly burnt; not sure how that happened. The doc puts the time of death at around midnight last night.'

Page touched a finger on the area of the burn. He leant low, bringing his face close to that of the deceased and sniffed deeply. He stood up. 'Strange that, no smell of spirits or petrol.'

'Looks like someone had a grudge,' Godley said.

'Or tried to hide the identity. I've seen that done before, lad.' He straightened up and took a pace back from the body, eying it critically. 'Certainly *looks* like Donovan. Anything in his pockets to say who he is?'

'No, sir. There was a wallet with a ten bob note in it and three shillings and sixpence ha'penny loose in his pockets. There was a train ticket as well: return half to Canterbury. That's it.'

'Well, we fingerprinted Donovan when he was arrested. As soon as they do the post mortem, get the corpse fingerprinted. That'll give us a positive identification.'

*

The muster room at the police station was humming with suppressed conversations. Off-colour remarks flew around like bats in a midnight boneyard. Laughs were stifled; reduced to sniggers. The sergeant was getting a dressing down.

In Page's office the desk sergeant stood stiffly to attention. Page's humour hovered between sarcasm and fury.

'So what's your explanation, man?'

'It was a mistake, sir.'

'A mistake. I'll give you a mistake, Sergeant. I'd say it was more like carelessness, delinquency; that's what I'd call it. Mistake, indeed. I might just mistakenly give you the sack, Sergeant – with your marching orders in it. How did this *mistake*, as you put it, occur?'

The sergeant's face had turned a florid puce. He wasn't used to being on the wrong end of a rough tongue; it was usually him handing out the harsh words. 'We were tidying up the files, sir. Getting rid of excess paperwork.'

'*You were tidying up!*' Page snorted the words, all but choking on them.

'We're short of space, sir.'

'Short of brains more like it.'

'I'm sorry, sir. It was a genuine error.'

'You can say *that* again! Rule one of proper procedure, Sergeant: preserve the evidence. Even when the case is closed, always preserve the evidence. You can never be sure there won't be an appeal, or the case reopened. It's an absolute fundamental. Destroy nothing; keep everything until some judge somewhere tells you it's OK. That goes for fingerprints. Especially for fingerprints. *Did you not know that*!? How are we supposed to identify that corpse lying in the morgue? Well?'

'Sorry, sir. They got mixed up with some redundant papers. It was an accident.'

'Sergeant, consider yourself lucky that this station is so short-staffed. Otherwise you would be stripped down to constable and put on traffic direction. Get back to your post.'

'Sorry, sir.' The sergeant returned to the front desk, shoulders hunched with humiliation.

Page went testily to the muster room. He pulled the door open and stuck his head inside. 'Someone find Godley for me,' he growled.

Godley knocked and entered. He was followed by a uniformed constable carrying a tray with a pot of tea and two cups. 'On the desk, Constable.' Page pushed some papers to one side. 'Right, DC Godley, we have a small identity dilemma. We have a stiff, which is almost certainly our late friend, Henry Donovan – but nothing to evidence that being the case. Our administration sergeant just admitted he destroyed the file containing Donovan's fingerprints. Thirteen shillings and sixpence ha'penny and a return ticket to Canterbury will not stand up in front of a judge, Godley. Since we no longer have the print of his dabs, courtesy of our careless front office, what do you suggest we do, huh Godley? Your course of action?'

Godley poured tea into the two cups. 'Contact the next of kin would be usual, sir – but ...'

The Man at the Walpole Bay Hotel

'But we don't know who they might be. So what?'

Godley held up the milk jug questioningly.

Page nodded. 'Just a splash, Godley – and two sugars. So we do the next best thing. We find people who knew Donovan. Get them in for a visual identification. So, who do we know who was familiar with the deceased. Eh?'

Godley passed the tea to Page. 'Those two ladies who like playing sleuths. They were often in his company; and that young woman, the one whose room was turned over at the Walpole Bay; she seemed to be close to him.'

Page slurped at his tea cup. 'Better still, Godley, why don't we ask the cove who stood surety for Donovan's bail. You don't go sporting a monkey on a horse you don't know. Let's have him in and ask the question. The bail paper's in the front office. Get the address and pay him a visit. Let's do it right away, shall we.'

A short while later, DC Godley returned. 'That surety, he's at the Dalby Rooms Guest House, sir.'

'Right then, get on it, lad. When you find him, take him straight over to the morgue. Call me when you're on your way. I'll join you there.'

Half an hour later, the phone on Page's desk rang. He picked it up. It was the sergeant's voice, 'DC Godley, sir. He's says the bird has flown. He's on his way back.'

'Do we have any other address for the surety?'

'We do not, sir.'

The Man at the Walpole Bay Hotel

Minutes after Page had put the phone back on the hook, Godley poked his head round the door.

'Come in, lad. What's the story?'

'He left the guest house yesterday morning – early.'

'Any forwarding address?'

'He booked in as Mr S Trevelyan of 28 St James Street, London.'

'We should check it. I'll telephone Scotland Yard. Get someone to go round there.'

'I've already done that, sir. It's a gentleman's club at that address. Something called Boodles. I phoned them. They say they don't have a member by that name.'

Page pushed back on his chair. 'In that case it looks like a visit to the ladies. We do have an address for them – do we?'

Godley shuffled his feet. 'It appears we do not, sir.'

Page let his shoulders slump, a futile gesture of resignation. 'In that case we're left with Miss Lucinda Coates. Get over to the Walpole Bay Hotel and round her up, Godley.'

*

'Ah, here's the waiter. What do you say, Effie? Should we have tea and scones?'

'Oh rather – and with plenty of cream and strawberry jam. You do have strawberry jam, don't you, Herbert?'

The Man at the Walpole Bay Hotel

The waiter smiled. 'Of course, Mrs Dalrymple, and very good it is too. Made locally from wild strawberries.'

'That sounds perfect', Dorothy interjected. 'We shall have it out here on the veranda.

'Isn't that one of those policemen?' she said, quickly changing the subject and pointing to a man who was climbing the front steps and heading in the direction of the reception. 'That detective constable who trails around after Inspector Page? He looks dreadfully young for that job. More like a schoolboy.'

Effie laughed. 'Well, you know what they say. When the policemen look young it's because we are getting old.'

'I wonder what he's doing here,' Dorothy said in a voice that showed little more than passing interest.

'Perhaps he wants to talk to Lucy about that break-in.'

'Well, we shall soon find out. Look. Here they come.'

Effie stopped pouring tea and placed the pot back on its stand. Seeing them, Lucinda left DC Godley and came over to the table. Her face looked quite pale and drained; she appeared to be trembling.

'Lucy, dear,' Dorothy said, 'whatever is the matter?'

'It's Harry, Aunt; this is so awful.' Her voice was cracked and the words came with difficulty.

Godley reached the table. 'I'm sorry to interrupt your afternoon tea, ladies, but I have asked Miss

The Man at the Walpole Bay Hotel

Lucinda to accompany me to the hospital. I'm afraid I shall have to ask you to come along as well.'

Dorothy raised an indignant eyebrow. 'Good gracious, whatever for, young man?'

'There's been a death and I shall need you to help with the identification of the deceased.'

'It's Harry, Aunt Dorothy; they say he's been found dead. It's dreadful.' Her words were choked off and she began to cry.

'*Dead!*' Dorothy and Effie chorused in unison. 'How, dead?' Dorothy insisted. 'Where? When did this thing happen?'

'Last night, about midnight, madam. He was found out back of the George Hotel, in the stable yard. The coroner's doctor says he'd had a regular skinful to drink. It could have been an accident – but we can't rule out foul play.'

Dorothy frowned. 'Well, we can't just abandon these scones, you know. Sit down, Lucy dear; Effie will pour you a soothing cup of tea. Maybe you should have a shot of cognac in it. You look quite wan. Constable, go to the bar and ask the waiter to bring a shot. Then I suggest you wait in the reception lobby until we are ready for you. There are some nice comfortable armchairs there. Now, go along.'

*

'Hmm, I recognise that smell,' Dorothy said, and wrinkled her nose. 'They all use the same disinfectant, you know. You can tell a mortuary the world over. Night-scented stocks. Even when we were in India it was the same. I used to accompany George sometimes, when there was a tricky post mortem. I used to take notes for him.'

They stood in an austerely decorated room with no more furniture than a desk and two chairs.

A mortician in a white coat wheeled in a trolley. It was covered with a grey rubber sheet, the profile of the body clearly visible beneath it. The three women stood to one side, with DC Godley. Page, meanwhile, had moved to the head of the trolley

The mortician stood gravely in attendance. 'Inspector Page,' he said sombrely, 'when everyone is ready, please.'

Page nodded. 'One at a time if you would be so good, ladies.'

Lucinda was shaking as she stepped forward, Godley steadying her with a hand on her elbow.

'I just want you to take a quick look when the sheet is drawn back and tell me if you recognise the person underneath.' Page gestured to the mortician, who pulled back the rubber sheet to expose the face and neck of the corpse. Lucinda let out a short moan and crumpled at the knees.

'She's going. Catch her, Godley!' Page barked.

Godley stepped forward but Lucinda had already recovered. She looked at Page but said nothing.

'Well?' Page said.

Lucinda nodded, but still said nothing.

'Take Miss Coates out, Godley – find her somewhere to sit down, and a cup of tea. Now, Mrs Dalrymple.' He looked at Effie as if she

The Man at the Walpole Bay Hotel

might be frail. 'Do you think you are up to it, madam?'

Effie smiled. 'Oh, how thoughtful of you, but don't worry. I've seen a lot of dead bodies. My husband and I were at Mafeking, you know. We were under siege. 217 days. I helped out in the hospital; dressing the dead and popping them into coffins. There were an awful lot of them. Some were quite dreadfully rotten. The weather was very hot you see. I remember one poor soul; when we picked him up, one of his legs dropped off ...'

Page put up a hand. He'd heard quite enough. 'Very well. Please come and stand by the mortician.' The sheet was pulled back. Effie took a long hard look.

'Well,' she eventually said, 'he is a bit charred around the gills – but – yes, I think that certainly looks like him. What do you think, Dorothy? Come and take a look.'

'One at a time, please ...,' Page had started to say, but Dorothy was already there, peering down at the burned face. 'Oh yes, I can see the similarity. Though I'm afraid he does look a bit like an overdone sirloin ... and he had nothing about his person, Inspector; to give a clue to who he was?'

'Thirteen shillings and sixpence ha'penny, and the return portion of a rail ticket.'

'A rail ticket. Where was he returning to?'

Page puffed impatiently. 'Canterbury, madam. Now, please, is this in your opinion Henry Donovan?'

'Regrettably, I think I probably have to say yes.'

The Man at the Walpole Bay Hotel

Page gave a sigh of relief and indicated to the mortician that they were done. 'Now, ladies, I suppose you would like a cup of tea?'

Dorothy looked at her watch, and then at Effie, who gave her a knowing look. She shrugged at Page. 'I rather think a cocktail would be more appropriate to the hour, Inspector. We shall go to the Walpole Bay Hotel – would you care to join us for a snifter?'

Page just stood there slowly glancing from one to the other, eyebrows raised. 'Thank you, ladies, not while I'm on duty.'

'He is a dreadfully stuffy man, do you not think?' Dorothy said as they arrived at the Walpole Bay Hotel. 'All this talk of duty. He would never have got by in the army, I can tell you. Ah good, there's Simpson. A gin and Italian for me I think, if you please, Simpson. What about you, Effie?'

'I think I might like to try something different,' Effie said, grinning impishly. 'What can you suggest, Simpson?'

'I have recently heard from a guest that there is a certain Mr Straub in America who has published a slim volume of cocktail recipes. I understand he loaned it to our new barman, Mr Robson. Robson highly recommends something called an Astoria.'

'What's in it, Simpson?'

'All manner of things, Mrs Coates. There is gin, orange bitters, apple brandy – I believe also an olive and a twist of lemon.'

'I must say that sounds good,' Dorothy grinned. What say you, Effie?'

The Man at the Walpole Bay Hotel

'Well it has been a rather trying afternoon. What with burnt bodies and poor Lucy going all faint like that.'

'Quite so. Better make them stiff ones, Simpson.'

*

Dorothy woke early to thoughts of the previous day nagging in her brain. The death of Henry Donovan had raised questions for which she presently had no answers. 'Do we have the morning paper, Muggers?'

'We do, Mrs Coates.'

The housekeeper put a rack of toast and two lightly boiled eggs on the table. 'I'll get it right away,' she said, then hustled off to find it.

'There's a picture of that dead man on the front page, madam' she informed Dorothy as she came back into the room. 'Sounds like he met a nasty end.'

Dorothy took a slice of toast from the rack and carefully buttered it. 'Yes, it was rather unpleasant. Put the paper down next to the toast rack, thank you Muggers.'

As she dug a finger of toast into the first egg she ran her eyes across the printed image of Donovan. 'You knew something you weren't telling us, Harry,' she muttered to the picture between bites of toast. 'Who were you, and what were you up to? Did you really do for Benedict Grayson – and if so, why? What was the motive? And who did for you, Harry?' The picture stared back at her, blankly. It gave no answers. Then a thought struck her.

When she had finished eating she picked up the phone and placed a call. 'Effie, I'm coming over to see you. I've had an idea. We should discuss it.'

*

'Hey ho, Effie, we are going to Canterbury. I have an errand,' Dorothy called down the hallway as soon as Freida opened the front door.

'That's nice. I love shopping in Canterbury,' Effie called back. 'Shall we take the train?'

'No, I want to go in the Prince Henry.'

'Would not the train be more convenient?'

Dorothy waved the idea away. 'Not for what I have in mind – and it isn't shopping. We may need to rove far beyond the town centre. Besides, public transport is so – mmm, public; and much of the time the public does not know how to conduct itself.'

Effie frowned and gave her a stern look. 'Well, all I can say is I hope you are not going to drive the whole way like a demon possessed.'

'Now, don't be a crosspatch, Effie. The open road, a blue sky and the wind in our hair; we shall have a positively splendid jaunt.'

The road out of town was quiet and after ten minutes they passed through Birchington. 'Why are we going to Canterbury?' Effie asked, as the

The Man at the Walpole Bay Hotel

Prince Henry gathered speed. 'Only, you didn't say. Just that it wasn't shopping.'

'A missing person, Effie. We are going to try to track down a missing person.'

'Oh,' Effie responded, but said no more as the rushing sound of the air from their slipstream drowned out any hope of further conversation.

'Excellent,' Dorothy announced as the Prince Henry turned in through the West Gate of the city. 'Pound Lane. This is what we want.' She pulled the car to a halt in front of a solid looking stone building with gothic arched windows, and a heavy oak door. The sign above it announced POLICE STATION.

Inside, the lobby was extensive, with a flagstone floor and a lofty vaulted ceiling. 'Makes Margate jail look like a bit of a tiddler,' Effie remarked.

The lobby presented a scene of busy movement with constables, clerks, and men who by their dress were clearly solicitors, all passing back and forth, each one with an air of earnest endeavour etched on their faces.

Sitting on a bench at one side of the room, a rough-looking man, dressed in the striped clothing of an inmate of Canterbury prison, gazed vacantly at the floor; handcuffed and chained in leg irons. He scowled at them and they gave him a wide berth.

Dorothy led the way to the enquiries desk, where a sergeant and two constables stood in attendance.

'Ladies?' One of the constables said in a questioning tone. 'How may I be of assistance?'

'I want to know,' Dorothy launched in, 'if you have had a report of a missing person in the last day or two?'

'Is there a name, madam?'

'Possibly, but that may not be helpful. So any missing person will do for the moment.'

The constable looked confused. 'These things are filed by name, madam.'

'Very well. Try Henry Donovan, though that may not be his real name.'

The constable raised his eyebrows. 'I'll see what I can find. It might take a few minutes.' He left the counter and disappeared down a corridor. About a quarter of an hour later, he returned, shaking his head. 'Nothing I'm afraid. Sorry to disappoint you, ladies.'

'Ah, well yes, that is disappointing,' Dorothy said, heaving a noisy sigh.

Hearing her remark, the sergeant in charge of the enquiry desk leaned towards her. 'What is the problem, madam?'

'These ladies are enquiring about a missing person, Sarg,' the constable butted in. 'Trouble is we don't have a name. I've looked through all the cases. There's nothing fits their description, though. Male, slim build, tall, about six foot, dark hair and a full set of whiskers Age around thirty.'

The sergeant thought for a moment. 'Wasn't there one like that this morning? Woman came in to report a missing husband.' He produced a ledger marked 'Daily Reports' from under the counter and opened it. He ran a finger down the page. 'Yes, there we are. A Mrs Sanderson. He tapped a finger on the entry. 'Her husband, Henry Sanderson. Salesman, on the road; been out for a couple of weeks. Should have returned home three days ago – except that he didn't. Do you have information regarding his whereabouts?'

'I'm not sure,' Dorothy said. 'Could you give me the address for Mrs Sanderson? I think I should like to talk with her.'

'Can't do that I'm afraid, ladies; against regulations. I can take a message for her if you wish. Though I can't say when she might get it. Sorry.'

Dorothy pondered the offer. 'No, not to worry,' she eventually said. 'Thank you anyway. Good afternoon.'

Back in the Prince Henry, Dorothy huffed her irritation at coming so close but not getting an address for the woman. 'We could try the local library. She may be registered there. Or the council offices. If he is a property owner then he will be on their register. There must be some way to find the address.'

'Oh, that's not a problem,' Effie grinned. 'It was in that policeman's book. I got used to reading things upside down when we were in Berlin. It was a sort of hobby, you could say. Silly really, but it passed the time. Our Mrs Sanderson lives in St Radigund's Street. I have the number too.'

'I say, well done, Effie. Why don't we pay a visit. Perhaps we can get to the bottom of our Mr Donovan – or is that Sanderson – notice the similarity; both called Henry as well. Married too,

The Man at the Walpole Bay Hotel

that's a bit naughty of him to be playing around with dear Lucy. Bit of a bounder by all accounts.'

The house in St Radigund's Street was modest: a terraced two-up two-down. The woman who opened the door, however, was not a match for the very ordinary house. She looked quite sensuous, clearly of Latin origin, with exotically pale olive skin and jet-black hair that matched the colour of her eyes. When she spoke, the voice was richly Italianate. She dripped with the glitter of jewellery. At first, when she opened the door, she looked askance at the two women standing there.

'Mrs Sanderson?' Dorothy asked.

The look turned to one of suspicion. 'Si – Wha'dya want?'

'It's about your husband. May we come in and talk to you?'

The woman did not reply. She studied the two standing on her doorstep, weighing them up. After a few seconds she jerked her head at the hallway. 'Si, okay.'

She took them into a small front room which, like the woman, was also extravagantly over-decorated. The furniture was continental, the upholstery fine silk brocade, as were the curtains. There was a gilded French clock, which dwarfed the tiled mantle on which it sat; ridiculing the curiously small cast-iron grate beneath.

She invited them to sit down. 'So,' she said aggressively without waiting for the nicety of any introduction, 'which foolish little girl has he got into trouble this time? Heh? *Il stronzo di putana.*'

The Man at the Walpole Bay Hotel

'I don't think you understand ... ,' Effie had started to say, but she was cut short by a string of Italian expletives ending with, 'And do not ask me to pay for *'is stoopeed* games. I 'ad enough already. *Alora – tutti e finito.* Anyways, ee is gone. Ee don't come back when ee should. I told police. You wanna 'im, you look. So!' She finished with a flourish of her hands and the rattle of gold bracelets.

Dorothy took a folded newspaper from her bag and spread it open to show the front-page picture of Donovan. 'Is this your husband?'

The woman gave it a cursory glance. '*Si, bastardo*!'

Dorothy started to fold the paper but the woman put out a hand and took it from her. She looked more intently at the picture, then handed the paper back. 'No. Not 'im. My *stronzo* ee 'av what you call a mole. Right 'ere.' She jabbed a finger at the right cheek, just below the eye. 'This one ee maybe look like 'im, but – no! Ee not 'im.'

'What did you think of that?' Dorothy laughed as they drove back along the road to Margate.

'Mrs Sanderson?'

'Yes.'

Effie grinned mischievously. 'Like an over-decorated Christmas tree.'

'Yes. Still, a very successful foray. Cocktails when we get back to the Walpole. I think we've earned it.'

'I suppose we should tell Inspector Page when we get back that his corpse isn't Harry after all.'

'Well we can't be sure, but, if the body in the mortuary has a mole then it is Sanderson – and if that is the case, it does beg the question: where is Harry?'

They were twelve miles from Margate when Dorothy pulled to a halt at the side of the road. She took off her driving gloves and tapped on one of the dials on the dashboard. 'Drat it!' She tapped on it again, this time more vigorously. 'Just as I thought.'

Effie looked anxiously at the meaningless scattering of dials that studded the car's dashboard. 'What is it? Nothing serious I hope?'

'Not yet, I think – though it would be if I hadn't noticed it. It's the fuel gauge; the needle sometimes sticks. It was reading half full till I rapped on it. That kicked it into life. Look, we're actually knocking on empty. In that glove box, Effie, the cubby hole just to your left. There's a copy of the Automobile Association member's handbook. A very handy compendium it is too. It lists a whole variety of useful things, including locations where petrol is to be purchased.'

She took the book and flicked through the pages. 'We're in luck, Effie. There is a petrol pump in the village of St Nicholas at Wade, which is barely a mile from here.'

The village was little more than a church, a handful of houses and two pubs. 'There,' Effie called out pointing to where a single petrol pump stood on a paved court in front of a mechanic's workshop; just next door to a public house.

'Fill her up, please,' Dorothy instructed a man who had emerged from the workshop. He cranked on the handle of the mechanical pump and fuel gushed noisily into the empty tank. While that was being done, Dorothy took the notion that it might be a good idea to inspect the engine oil level. She walked round to the front of the Prince Henry where she proceeded to unlatch the engine cover. In the same moment she glanced across the street to where her eye caught sight of two men who were standing outside the Bell Inn, across the way. 'Effie,' she said in a quietly measured tone. 'Look. It's those two. The Fenians. What do you suppose they are doing here?'

Before Effie could answer, another event caught their attention. A large black Rolls Royce limousine drew up in front of the pub.

'There's only one man who has a motor like that around these parts,' Dorothy murmured. 'Ratty.'

After a minute or two of conversation with the driver, the two Fenians drained their beer glasses, left them on the table, and got into the Rolls.

'I have to have a word with Ratty,' Dorothy said after she had paid the man for the petrol. 'He's keeping bad company again.'

The Rolls started to move, with the men still in it. Dorothy waited until the limousine was out of sight then set off in the same direction. 'Now what?' she said as they reached the edge of the village. 'Over there. Do you see?'

The Man at the Walpole Bay Hotel

The Rolls Royce had left the road and turned up a track which led to a large barn.

Dorothy slowed the Prince Henry to no more than a walking pace, then stopped behind the cover of a hedgerow. 'Come on,' she said. 'Let's get a closer look.'

The two women worked their way back towards the track until they reached a point where they had to stop, or they would lose their cover and be exposed.

Three men emerged from the Rolls. One hauled open the door of the barn and they all disappeared inside.'

'Do you think we should we take a closer look?' Effie said, almost under her breath, though they were too far away for even a normal voice to be heard.

'No, we'd be too easily seen. I think we should come back later. When it's dark.'

*

In Margate police station, Page got up from his desk, put on his jacket, and headed for the front desk and the street outside. He stuck his head into the muster room where his DC was drinking tea and chatting with a group of constables.

'I've had a call from that Mrs Coates, Godley.' I'm going over to the morgue. She and that other woman say they need to look at the stiff again. Say they need to be sure they've made the right decision about it being Donovan.'

'Do you want me to accompany you, sir?'

The Man at the Walpole Bay Hotel

'No, I can handle it. Not much chance of them having a fit of the vapours and falling over. Hard boiled those two.'

'So, why do they want to see it again. Did they say?'

'They did not, lad. Imaginary sleuths those two. That's the trouble with these ladies of leisure. Too much time on their hands. No doubt they will be endowed with some crackpot theory which I shall have to listen to. I look forward to a nice cuppa when I get back. I shall definitely be in need of it.'

*

In the mortuary, they stood together at the head of the trolley once more. This time Page had not bothered to separate them. 'Right-ho,' he said to the mortician. The cover was pulled back. Both women leant forward. Dorothy went to put out a hand to the face of the corpse.

'Don't touch please, Mrs Coates. Only look.'

'I need to feel for something. The face is too charred for me to see properly.' Page looked to the mortician. The man nodded.

'Very well, but keep it brief.'

Dorothy ran her finger over the cheek, just under the right eye. 'It's there all right,' she told Effie. 'Feel for yourself.'

'All right, ladies, this is not a free-for-all. That's enough. What's this about anyway?'

Dorothy looked Page straight in the eye. 'This corpse is *not* Mr Donovan. It is a Mr Henry Sanderson, of Canterbury. His wife reported him missing yesterday. I suggest you get in contact with the desk sergeant at Canterbury police station. He knows all about it. I don't know who killed him, or why – but I do know this is *not* Henry Donovan.'

Effie just stood there giving little corroborating nods as Dorothy trotted out the story of their discovery. Page confined himself to saying, 'I see,' at appropriate moments in the narrative, though when she started to lay out a possible theory that she had now formed concerning both this death and that of Benedict Grayson, Page held up a hand. 'I'm sure it's most interesting, Mrs Coates, but I have to get back to the station. Thank you for your time, and the information. Now I must go.'

'You know, Dorothy,' Effie said after they left the morgue. 'I don't think Inspector Page was terribly pleased with our news.'

'He is a man most fixed in his ideas. Especially when it comes to solving crimes. Now, about that barn over at Saint Nicks. I think our *modus operandi* should be to have dinner at The Bell Inn, and then when the sun goes down pop over and take a peek inside. I took the opportunity to talk to the man at the petrol pump. He assures me they do a very good roast beef at The Bell. What do you say?'

Effie nodded her agreement. 'I think that is a very sound plan Dorothy. It doesn't get dark until about half nine, but if we were to give ourselves an hour we could be back to the Walpole in time for a nightcap.'

*

'We shall both have the roast beef with Yorkshire pudding,' Dorothy said to the waiter, 'and a nice bottle of Burgundy I think.' She hesitated until he had gone before asking Effie, 'Did you bring the Mauser with you?'

'No,' Effie said apologetically. 'Should I have, do you think?'

Dorothy nodded sagely. 'Probably best if one goes armed on expeditions like this.'

'Do you think it might be dangerous then?'

'Only if we are discovered. One can never tell with people like this lot. They are a rather unsavoury crew.'

'It will be best, I think, if we do not walk up the track to the barn,' Dorothy suggested as they left the Bell Inn, 'just in case there are occupants. An oblique approach will be best. But first we must get our kit. It's in the back of the Prince Henry.'

'What kit is that?' Effie said, slightly mystified.

'This,' Dorothy hissed under her breath, as they arrived at the Prince Henry. She heaved a leather bag of the sort that doctors carry, out of the back of the car. 'Tools of the trade.'

'What tools?'

'A small jemmy and a torch. It's what burglars carry you know. We shall almost certainly have to break in.'

'Yes, I suppose we shall. I hadn't thought of it like that – we shall be burglars; how exciting.'

Under the dim light of a half-moon they picked their way through a field of turnips; the silhouette of the barn was a dark shadow on the horizon. When they were only yards from the building, Dorothy held up a hand, then put a finger to her lips. They waited, standing motionless. In the stillness the only sound was the mournful hooting of a tawny owl, calling from somewhere back in the trees.

Dorothy started to move again. 'Not the front door,' she whispered. 'If we break the lock they will know someone has been here. We should go round the side. I want to see if there is another way in; a window perhaps.'

They had walked the length of the building but there were no windows, just a loading hatch at loft height. Dorothy shone the torch on it. 'Too high,' she said in a hushed voice. They moved on. At the back of the barn they ran into a thick screen of shrubs and weeds growing tight up against the wood planking of the walls. Dorothy shone the torch over it, right and left, looking for the one chance she thought might present itself.

'This is what we want, Effie.' Dorothy shone the torch on a crack where one of the planks had become dislodged, the heads on the securing nails having rusted away. She slipped the nose of the jemmy into the gap and levered on its swan neck. The plank peeled back with barely a sound. She applied the jemmy to a second one and that too gave up without complaint. 'One more, I think,' she said under her breath, 'then we're in.'

The third plank resisted. Its nails were sound and the board squeaked and groaned as it fought to stay in place. Grudgingly, it began to give way. Dorothy heaved harder on the tail of the jemmy. There was a splintering sound. She stopped. The board was cracking. She had to give up. If the board broke it would be clear someone had been in. She looked at the gap left by the other two boards, which now lay on the ground. 'I think we might just squeeze through. Shall we try?'

'Yes, I think we should,' Effie whispered. 'It would be a pity to come so close only to give up. Let me go first; I'm smaller than you.'

Inside, the part of the barn they had entered was filled with newly cut straw sheaves, all neatly tied into bundles and stacked. Beyond them was a combined reaper-binder, and next to that, rails of horse tack and harnesses, then a sledge harrow and a mechanical hoe. At the far end they came upon a Ford truck with a tarpaulin back.

'None of this looks very sinister.' Dorothy sounded disappointed.

'What did we hope to find? You didn't say.'

'I wasn't sure, to be honest, Effie. It just seemed likely there would be something, allowing that those two Fenians and Ratty had a rendezvous here. Ratty is not a man to waste his time on socialising. With him there's always something changing hands for money. So, what were they doing here?'

'I suppose we should go,' Effie said, clearly sharing the disappointment.

Dorothy swung the beam of the torch around the space and then up into the void of the roof. 'Nothing but what a farmer might have need of,' she admitted glumly. She shone the beam onto the bonnet of the Ford truck. 'Model T, Effie. Not very exciting but a good workhorse. And cheap too. Farmer's friend this thing.' She pulled idly at the tarpaulin cover and lifted one corner. The edge of a box caught her eye.

'Effie, hold the torch, if you please. I want to take a look under here.' She peeled back the canvas cover. For a moment she said nothing. Then a low whistle. 'Jackpot, Effie. By George, it's the jackpot.'

'What is it?'

Dorothy took the torch and played it across the cargo of boxes. She found one that had been opened and lifted the lid. 'No mere bagatelle, this little lot.'

'But what's in them?'

'Guns, Effie. Lots and lots of guns. Come along, it's time we left.'

Outside, they lifted the planks into place and tapped them back onto the old nail shanks.

'Right,' Dorothy said, looking at her watch when they reached the Prince Henry. 'Walpole Bay for a nightcap I rather think. If we don't spare the horses we should make it in time.'

The Man at the Walpole Bay Hotel

'Tally-ho,' Effie giggled, 'and I shan't complain if you put your foot down on this one.'

*

On the following morning, Page strode up the steps of the Walpole Bay Hotel; DC Godley one step behind him. He marched through the lobby and presented himself at the reception desk. 'I want to see your guest; that Mr Donovan. Is he still here?'

The receptionist looked flustered at the abruptness of the demand. He consulted the guest register. 'No, sir; he left two days ago.'

'Did he leave an onward address?'

'No, sir.'

'What address did he give when he registered on his arrival?'

The receptionist turned the book around to face Page. 'This one, sir.'

Page gave a shrug. '28 St James Street, Godley. We already know that's bogus.'

From behind him he became aware of his name being called. It was a female voice, and unmistakeable. Page turned and saw what he hoped he wouldn't. 'Oh my good Lord,' he groaned. 'Spare me from the well-meaning and the idly curious.'

It was too late to avoid them. Dorothy and Effie bore down on Page and Godley.

'Are we going to tell him about the barn and the guns?' Effie whispered just before they reached the two men.

'No,' Dorothy hissed. 'Not yet. Tell you why later.'

'Good day to you, ladies,' Page said sourly. 'Here for your lunch, are you?'

'As a matter of fact, yes,' Dorothy said, 'but since we saw you were here too, I thought I might enquire if you had made any progress with this new murder. Have you spoken to the Canterbury police by the way? I hope that was useful.'

Page forced a grudging smile. 'Yes, thank you. It did help in the identification of the man – but what makes you suppose that he was murdered?'

'It's in the report being prepared for the coroner: damage to the trachea and pharynx – probable cause, a ligature, it says. Mr Sanderson was strangled.' Effie was nodding furiously in agreement.

Page almost choked with indignation at that. 'The report hasn't been published yet, how ...'

'It was lying open on the mortician's desk,' Dorothy said, cutting him short.

'I read it,' Effie smiled. 'I read upside down writing, you see.'

Page had taken to shaking his head. He raised his eyebrows at Godley, who responded with a barely susceptible shrug of his shoulders. There was nothing to say; he had no answers.

'All I can say at the moment, ladies, is that there are indications that foul play might be involved here. No more than that. And I should caution you that obtaining access to police documents without the proper authority could be construed as an offence; especially in these times when there's a war on.'

Dorothy offered a patronising smile, as if admonishing a naughty child. 'Well, it was rather carelessly left lying about, you know, Inspector. But don't worry, we shan't tell.'

'I don't suppose you would know the whereabouts of Mr Donovan, by any chance,' Godley cut in, trying to cover the embarrassment of his chief.

Effie looked at Dorothy. 'I don't think we do – do we?'

'No – but if we should hear anything, Inspector, you will be the first person we shall tell. Now, it *is* time for our luncheon. Shall we go to the dining room, Effie?'

Page looked relieved to see them go. 'Saved by the lunch gong, Godley. Dear lord, preserve me from busy women.'

'An aperitif before lunch I think, Effie.'

'A fine notion, why not. Oh, I say, look at that.' Effie pointed to an overflowing ashtray on the bar. 'That needs clearing away, Robson,' she said to the barman.

'Of course, madam, my apologies.' He went to pick up the offending ashtray but Dorothy put out a hand. 'Well, I never.' She picked a barely smoked cigarette out of the debris. 'Look at that.'

'What is it?' Effie looked puzzled.

'You see the little image printed on this cigarette?'

'I do. It's a horse.'

The Man at the Walpole Bay Hotel

'No, it's a camel. An American cigarette as we know. I think, Effie, that our mysterious American is back in Margate. Mr Jackson Molloy of Boston. Now what's he doing here? Robson, do we have any American guests staying?'

'We did have, ladies. A gentleman. Only here for one night; he left yesterday. What will you have?'

'Well, those Astorias you made were rather good. How about that?'

Effie nodded with enthusiasm. 'That sounds rather splendid.'

Chapter 13

A trip to London

'What are you thinking about?' Effie said while they waited for the menus to be brought to the table. 'I always know when you are thinking – your face gets a rather rumpled look. I shouldn't imagine it is too good for the skin, you know. I'm sure it will bring on early wrinkles – and you don't want that. I would advise that you think less. Ah, good, here are the menus. Ooh, they have fresh turbot with parsley sauce, I think I shall have that. Now, as I was saying – what are you thinking about?'

'I was thinking, Effie, that we should take a trip to London.'

'That would be nice – but why?'

Dorothy's face assumed a serious look. 'Harry, Effie – Harry Donovan. We need to find him. He is the one missing piece in my jigsaw puzzle. I think I have most of the rest of the pieces in place.'

'But we don't have an address – do we?'

'No, but it's clear to me that we have to stop pithering about and instead we must become proper detectives. We must track him down. I am sure he holds the missing piece. I just don't know what it is. Harry *is* important. I think Inspector Page has come to that conclusion too, though I think for entirely another reason. That policeman is still barking up the wrong tree in my opinion.'

'But I still don't understand how we are going to find Harry without an address. London is a very big place. Mind you, there is Mr Harrod's store if we fail to find Harry. No point in a wasted journey.'

Dorothy shook her head and gave her friend a severe finger wagging. '*No shopping*. At least not until we have accomplished our mission. Right, now where was I? Oh yes, detection. Lucy has a friend working in the British Library. We know the Fenians were there, and also the German. That is where we should start. We need to find the first thread. I shall speak with Lucy; we need to have a proper introduction to her friend if we are going to ask her for confidential cooperation.'

'I say, that's really clever of you, Dorothy. You would make a jolly good detective.'

'Thank you, Effie. Now let me see what else is on today's menu. You're probably right about the turbot. How about we have a decent Chablis to go with it?'

'Agreed.'

*

'I'm rather glad I left the Prince Henry in Margate,' Dorothy commented as their train pulled into St Pancras. 'I do not like London traffic. There are still far too many horse-drawn conveyances blocking up every street; and then there are the omnibuses, the taxis, the motor lorries – and bicycles. It is positively mayhem, and the air smells so foul.'

'Indeed,' Effie agreed, holding a lace handkerchief to her nose, 'and you wouldn't be doing any speeding here with all this traffic, that is most certain. How far is the Library from here? Shall we walk – or should we take a taxi?'

'Neither,' Dorothy said emphatically. 'The new electric underground is said to be most agreeable and the quickest way to cross the capital.'

'I'm not too fond of confined spaces,' Effie said anxiously. 'However, if needs must, then needs it shall be. Lead on.'

They emerged into Russell Square where they encountered the plodding clatter of horseshoes on paving, the honk of motor horns and the all-pervading London smell: a mix of motor exhaust, dung and stale horse urine.

From one corner a paperboy shouted his wares together with the headlines: *British Expeditionary Force and French retreat; Paris at risk.*

'I must say that doesn't sound promising,' Dorothy remarked as they reached the entrance to the British Museum. 'We shouldn't be downhearted, but I am not sure it *will* all be over by Christmas. Right, onwards to the Library.'

Effie took a deep breath through her nose, sniffing the musty air of the room as they entered. 'I rather like the smell of books, don't you?'

'Yes, especially the leather bindings. Look, there's the person we need to speak to.' Dorothy motioned to where a studious-looking young woman sat at a central desk.

'Miss Blain?'

The woman looked up. 'Yes, how may I help?'

'I am the aunt of Lucinda Coates; she has written me this testimonial. I believe you may be able to assist me.' Dorothy handed her a folded paper note.

Miss Blain unfolded and read it. 'Of course,' she smiled. 'I am very pleased to make your acquaintance. What may I do to assist you?'

'I would like to look at your register of recent borrowers, if I may.'

'Please do; it is this journal here.' She opened a large book sitting on the desk and turned it round to face them.

Dorothy ran a finger down the list of entries. 'That's disappointing,' she said, shaking her head.

'Not there?' Miss Blain asked.

'No. I was hoping to find a name and an address for someone whom I know has visited recently.'

'Well, they might not have borrowed. Perhaps they simply browsed.' She moved another heavy tome towards the two women. 'If the person simply visited, then they will be noted in these pages.' She opened the new book. 'What name are we looking for?'

'Donovan, Mr Henry Donovan.'

There was a moment of silence while Miss Blain ran her eye down the columns. 'I'm afraid not,' she finally said.

'Now there's a name we know,' Effie coloured slightly at the sound of her own interruption. 'Sorry,' she added quickly. 'I read upside down, you know. It's a little foible of mine, but ... ,' she put a finger on an entry, '... Seymour Trevelyan.'

Dorothy gave a slow, meaningful nod. 'Now that *is* interesting.'

*

The address next to the name had directed them to a side road off Kensington Church Street. 'What now?' Effie asked as they stood in front of the door.

'The head-on approach is best in this case,' Dorothy said, rapping loudly with the knocker. After a moment it was opened. A middle-aged man stood there staring questioningly. 'Oh, I am sorry,' Dorothy hurriedly said. 'I've knocked on the wrong door. Do excuse us.'

They retreated back into the street and made off in the direction of Kensington Church Street. Effie looked puzzled. 'What was that about?'

Dorothy did not reply but instead hailed a taxi. 'Seymour Trevelyan,' she eventually said when they were comfortably installed in the back of the cab, 'I know who he is. *Now* I think I begin to understand almost everything.'

'Well, *do* tell. It all sounds most exciting.'

'I shall, Effie,' Dorothy looked down at the fob watch pinned to her coat lapel, 'but first I think we have earned a little refreshment.' She tapped on the driver's partition. 'Cabby, a change of plan. Do you know the store of Messrs Fortnum & Mason?'

'Of course, madam. Every taxi driver in London knows that one.'

'Then take us there, please.'

As they stepped into the tearoom, Effie sniffed affectionately at the air. 'I do so love the aroma of their coffee, though I think tea is in order for this hour of the day, is it not.'

'Oh, without question. A nice Darjeeling I think – or perhaps Lapsang?'

'The latter for me, and we should have cucumber sandwiches and perhaps fishpaste.'

Dorothy gave a smile of agreement. 'You know, the best paste in my view is to be had from Pegwell Bay. The shrimp paste from there is without equal – oh good, here's the waiter. A table for two if you please – and the tea menu.'

After they had been seated at a table, Effie could wait no longer. 'Now, come along Dorothy. Tell all. Who is this Seymour Trevelyan? And what's he got to do with the Margate business?'

'Well, I only met him twice, and he's a lot older now – but did you notice the scar on his left cheek?'

'Yes. The *first* thing I noticed. A duelling scar is what it looked like to me. They were common in Berlin, you know. Prussians mostly. They were a quarrelsome lot. Forever calling each other out at the simplest slight. Always with sabres, never pistols. Something to do with honour and etiquette, though I never quite understood it.'

Dorothy nodded. 'Some kind of military humbug, I believe.'

'Quite so. Oh, good, here's the tea. What a lovely cake stand, and I say just look at those cream fancies. We shall be thoroughly spoiled. Now, do have a sandwich, and tell me about this Trevelyan chap – and what's he got to do with Harry do you suppose.'

'Rather a lot I imagine.'

'So, don't keep me in suspense; tell all.'

'I met Seymour Trevelyan, or rather I was there when he came to see George. It was to have that cut on his face seen to. He was much younger then.'

'Weren't we all – but when exactly – how long ago?'

'A bit over thirty years now, back in the 1880s. I was a young gal and just married to George when Seymour turned up asking to have this gash sewn together. The circumstances were shady – no question about that. He claimed to have slipped and hit his face on a wall.'

Effie was agog. She put down her teacup. 'And had he?'

Dorothy shook her head. 'George thought not. He said it looked more like a knife wound. It was a clean cut, you see, not ragged as you would expect if he'd bumped his face as he'd claimed– and no grit or dirt in it. Just a deep, clean slice. Normally George would have shied from such a request, but he was only newly qualified and a subaltern in the medical corps. Army pay for junior officers did not go far, you see. It was before he was posted to India and there wasn't a lot of money, so he had to take on most anything. Seymour was quite definitely in the shadows. We thought him a tearaway and probably an adventurer to boot. After that we forgot about him until when we were in Calcutta and were invited to one of Lord Curzon's receptions in Government House – and who should be there, but Seymour Trevelyan.'

Effie drew in a deep breath. 'No!'

'Yes, there he was and, as bold as you like, he came up to George and whispered that he hoped no word of the incident of his cut face would enter any conversation, particularly should one arise with the Viceroy.'

'Well, bless my soul, that does *not* bode well.'

'Agreed, it does not.'

'But what of Harry?'

'What indeed? I now know where he fits in, and it is not what we had thought. It is now absolutely clear that he has been less than straightforward in his dealings with Lucy.'

The Man at the Walpole Bay Hotel

Effie carefully picked a cream and strawberry tart from the cake stand and took a small bite. She bunched up her shoulders and grinned cheekily at the indulgent delight. 'Definitely not good for the figure. I know I shall regret it, and my corset will be killing me by the end of the day … ,' she gave another guilty little shrug, '… but I just can't resist.'

Dorothy helped herself to a delicately cut triangle of white bread and fishpaste. 'So this is what I think our shady duo are up to in Margate …'

They left the tearoom and emerged onto Piccadilly. 'A taxi, I think,' Dorothy said, and headed briskly towards the spot where a queue of vehicles were lined up alongside the kerb. 'Hungerford Bridge, please, cabby,' she told the driver. 'The steamer pier. We should retrace what I believe were the steps taken by Harry when he came to Margate, Effie. He told Lucy he came on the paddler. We shall just be in time for the last sailing of the day.'

'Good idea,' Effie agreed as they climbed into the cab, 'but there are still things I don't understand in all of this.'

'Likewise, Effie dear, but you must admit the picture is becoming clearer. I'm hoping the trip down to the estuary might lend a clue or perhaps stir a memory. And there is little more pleasant than to sit out on the top deck with a drink. Such a civilised way to pass the journey.'

The Man at the Walpole Bay Hotel

'Quite so,' Effie agree, 'but I'm still in the dark over much of this. We know now that Harry wears a uniform other than the one in which he parades, and we know what his connection is to this Trevelyan man – but does that bring us any closer to why poor Mr Grayson was murdered?'

'I'm afraid not, Effie. That is still the dilemma.'

'Or, for that matter, that other fellow, Sanderson. Though, to be honest, I didn't much care for him; a mountebank and a philanderer, if the wife is to be believed. Of course, she *is* a foreigner, so one can never be quite certain.'

'True. Anyway, come along. We should go to the top deck and have a glass of something. It's a Pimm's sort of evening, wouldn't you say?'

'Ooh, I think so, without a doubt.'

*

'This thing is all getting rather messy, Harry.' Trevelyan went to a cabinet. He took out a bottle and waved it at Donovan. 'Whisky?'

'Thanks. Do you think they are onto us?'

'I suspect they are not far behind. Of course, they could become more of a nuisance than our flat-footed Inspector Page.'

'You said you knew Dorothy Coates.'

'Yes, we met briefly; long time ago, though. Doubt she'd remember me. Looks change, dear boy. Time trudges heavy-booted across all our faces, don'tcha know.'

The Man at the Walpole Bay Hotel

'Hmm, jolly awkward if she does, though. Bang goes my bird-watching story. Lucy would probably never speak to me again.'

'Would that matter to you, Harry?'

'Yes, I think it would.'

'Ha, do I detect the work of Cupid here? Formed an attachment to the girl, have we? Not a good idea, Harry – not for someone in your position.'

Chapter 14

Margate again

The *Canterbury Queen* cast off from its pier beneath Hungerford Bridge with the sound of two long hoots from the steam horn, then the thrashing noise of its paddle wheels churning the ebbing Thames water. The bow of the steamer slowly turned, moving the vessel towards the centre of the river where it picked up speed in the faster flowing current.

On the approach to Tower Bridge, the horn blasted out three long moaning hoots, and with the tide running with her, shot the bridge at a good eight knots, fairly racing past the bascules.

'I say, Dorothy, isn't that just the most splendid bridge in London?'

'It is rather majestic, I must agree. George took me to see the opening, you know; 1894. We were home on leave from Calcutta. Hardly seems any time since that day.

The Man at the Walpole Bay Hotel

'Now we should go to the bar and order our refreshments; then a waiter can bring them up to the top deck for us.'

'Splendid idea, Dorothy. We should find a seat forward of the smokestack, of course.'

'Oh, absolutely. I don't want to arrive in Margate covered in smuts and looking like the bib and apron of a song thrush. My goodness no – and I think we should review where we are with this case?'

'*Case*? My word, Dorothy, we *are* beginning to sound like proper detectives.'

'And why not? I believe we are closer than ever to solving this case. Come on, off to the bar; we shan't get that Pimm's by shilly-shallying around here.' Dorothy gave a flourish of her parasol and launched off in the direction of the main saloon.

'Do you mind if I desert you for a moment?' Effie announced after they had instructed both the barman and a waiter to attend to their needs. 'I think I shall go to the ladies room. I need to loosen my corset – before I pass out.'

Dorothy gently raised a hand of approval. 'Of course, my dear. Such a hostile garment. I don't know why we still wear the silly things. They are quite out of fashion in Paris, you know. I think I shall give up on mine.'

Effie giggled. 'Well if you do, then so shall I. After all, if we are to be proper detectives we need to move with the modern times.'

'Do you think Harry was actually there – in that house when we called?' Effie asked when they were settled with their Pimm's.

'Yes Effie, I do.'

'So, should we not have demanded to see him?'

'No, I don't think that would have resolved anything – other than letting him and Seymour Trevelyan know we were onto them.'

Effie nodded. 'Yes, of course, you are right. Now that we know who they are, and probably what they are up to, I suppose we should let sleeping dogs lie.'

'Indeed.' Dorothy said, looking out across the water. The estuary had begun to open up and the banks now looked quite far off. 'These paddlers fairly rush along when they're running with the tide. It's quite exhilarating …' She paused, then added, '… though I have to admit it has failed to provide me with little more than a pleasant afternoon.'

'No clues then?'

'Afraid not.'

'What were you expecting?'

Dorothy shook her head. 'Nothing really. I had just thought it might jog something.'

'And it didn't?'

'No, it didn't. There are still missing pieces. We have Harry and Trevelyan pinned like a couple of specimen beetles on a show board – but …'

'But?'

'But it still doesn't explain Benedict Grayson's death.'

Effie looked glumly down into her glass. 'Or who did it?'

'Well, that is not quite so. I think we have a prime suspect. You may recall from our conversation at Fortnum's.'

'Yes, of course. I must say it was a pretty good afternoon tiffin they served.'

*

The *Canterbury Queen* moored at the jetty in Margate where the crew heaved lines ashore to waiting dock hands. When she was securely tied off, the gangway was rolled into position and the passengers began to disembark. As she came down onto the jetty, Dorothy stopped. 'Fenians,' she said, without any precursor or prior explanation. 'It has to be them ... but why? Why would they need to kill both those men? I'm sure they did ... but why?'

Effie shrugged. 'Maybe the two men were connected somehow? It is a pity we can't just ask the Fenians. They must know.'

'True, but we can't. They already tried to kill us once, don't forget.'

'Maybe Ratty would know; after all, he seems to be in very thick with them. Those guns in the barn and all that.'

'Good idea, Effie. It can't do any harm. Now I think I shall walk home from here. I need to freshen up, wash the grit of London off my face. I'll telephone you later. We should lay some plans regarding how we deal with Ratty.'

As she approached the house, Dorothy stopped and stared. There was something not quite right. A policeman was standing on her doorstep. She marched up the steps to confront him. 'What is this about, Constable?!' Before he could answer, the front door opened. Her housekeeper stood there speechless for a moment, her face drawn with concern.

'Whatever is wrong, Muggers?'

'We've been burgled, Mrs Coates. Oh my Lord, the house has been burgled. I was out doing the shopping, you see, and when I came back – this is how I found it. I called the constables right away, madam. The thieves have made a terrible mess – everything has been turned upside down.'

Inside, it was plain to see. The place had been ransacked. Images of Lucy's burglary sprang into her mind. 'Is there anything missing, Muggers, do we know?'

Muggeridge quickly regained her composure. 'Not that I can tell, madam. That police inspector is here. He asked the same question. He's in the drawing room, madam.'

'Well, he's wasting his time in there. I'll wager a hundred to one I know what the thieves came for.' With that she stomped her way down the hall towards the library. 'Hello, Inspector, can't stop.' She threw the remark casually in through the door of the drawing room as she passed by, leaving Page no time to respond.

In the library she went directly to a roll-top bureau. Splintered wood around the lock told the story she had anticipated. All the drawers had been pulled open. 'I knew it,' she muttered quietly to herself, rustling through the mess of papers. 'I jolly well knew it,' she said again, this time out loud. 'Drat, and double drat.' She began to push the drawers back onto their runners.

'What was it you knew, Mrs Coates?' Page had caught up with her and was now standing in the doorway of the library.

'Too complicated, Inspector. Too much to explain.'

Page's face carried his usual hallmark of underwhelmed disinterest. 'I see, Mrs Coates. Well when you feel you have the time, and when you have ascertained whatever it is these toe rags have made off with, perhaps you would come to the station and make a report.' He raised his eyebrows and gave a vague shake of his head in the direction of a constable who had belatedly followed him to the study. 'I can have the constable stay while you re-order all this – if you are concerned that the miscreants might return.'

'No, but thank you for your concern, Inspector. They will not return – they have what they came for. Though much good it may do them. I shall be fine, thank you. The housekeeper will put everything back in its place.'

The Man at the Walpole Bay Hotel

Dorothy waited until Page and his constable had left then went straightway to the telephone.

'Effie, it's me, Dorothy. Have you still got a copy of that German document? The one you translated?'

'Yes.' The voice at the other end of the line held a note of wary anticipation. 'Why, has something occurred to you? You have a copy don't you?'

'No, Effie, not any longer. The house has been burgled. They've taken it.'

'Oh, good grief. Not Harry, do you suppose?'

'No, no. I'm jolly certain he was in London with Seymour.'

'Then who?'

'Fenians, dear girl – Fenians.'

'Well, what do you propose to do? I suppose you ought to report it to Inspector Page. He might be able to find the culprits. '

Dorothy suppressed the desire to laugh but it was there in her voice. 'I'm afraid any hope of that went down with the Titanic, dear girl. He was already here when I arrived home – and he looked thoroughly jiggered by the whole thing. Where he ever came by the name of Artful Archie has me completely fuddled. No, we shall have to work this one out for ourselves – over dinner. Always best to think on a full tummy. Why don't I drive over and collect you; we can get our usual table at the Walpole Bay. What say you?'

'An excellent idea. Eight o'clock?'

*

The Man at the Walpole Bay Hotel

'We have to find Ratty,' Dorothy said, at the same time nodding politely to the waiter who set down two wide-bowled glasses with sugar frosted rims in front of them. 'Compliments of Mr Robson, ladies. It's his new creation: the Walpole Bay Slammer. Says he'd be indebted for your expert opinion.'

'Oh, how very decent of him,' Effie said, holding her glass to the light. 'What a delightful colour. Just a hint of pink. What's in it – do we know?'

The waiter looked blank. 'Lord, madam, I don't. He won't tell – says it's a secret and how as you ladies are invited to try to guess it.'

Dorothy sniffed suspiciously at the rim of her glass, then took a genteel sip.

Effie had gone all wide-eyed with expectation. 'Well? Go on, tell me what you think. After all you are a detective now. You should analyse – you know, like Sherlock Holmes. That's how he solves his cases.'

Dorothy took another sniff. 'Hmm, quite clearly a hint of orange. I think orange bitters rather than a liqueur, and there is an underlying spirit. Clear, not perfumed so probably the Russian influence there. I get a faint notion of spice too, so possibly the Caribbean influence, hints of Jamaica there I rather think – a spiced rum perhaps. Finally there is a *pétillance* – surely that has to be champagne. So there you have my analysis. We shall have to enquire of Robson before we leave to see if my detection is up to the mark.'

Effie clapped a delicate applause.

The Man at the Walpole Bay Hotel

'Right, down to business,' Dorothy plucked the paper on which they had previously noted their clues, from her handbag. 'Now, let us consider what we have. Three murders, all seemingly disconnected, yet with common threads. Two happened in Margate, one in London – but the London death has a link to Margate through Harry, because the German was a known associate, and Harry came to Margate.'

'Though not to study wading birds, as we now know,' Effie proposed.

'Quite so. Then we have Seymour Trevelyan, who is clearly in cahoots, as our American cousins would express it.'

'And Jackson Molloy of Boston,' Effie added.

'Who we have seen talking to the Fenians, so must be included in the circle of associated persons – and we know they have been bringing guns ashore.'

'Which it looks like they are selling to Ratty.'

'Seemingly so – but ... ,' Dorothy let go a deep sigh and held out both hands, for all the world like a priest administering extreme unction; a last blessing to the departing soul, '... however that may add up to little more than a doubtful side transaction. So, in short, though we have all these threads, we are still not much closer than Inspector Page in understanding why the two Margate murders occurred.

'In the case of the German, it is clear; he was in on the gun-running business, and the Fenians probably did for him. I suspect he may have been blackmailing them. Those papers you translated

The Man at the Walpole Bay Hotel

tell us most of what we need to know in that case. But Benedict Grayson … ?' Dorothy shrugged, '… where does he fit in? And that awful bounder, from Canterbury – Sanderson? You know, Effie, this detecting business is turning out to be a lot harder than I supposed it might be.'

'It is very vexing, I grant you.'

'Tomorrow we should seek out Ratty. He knows something, of that I am sure. And I want to know more about the person he saw the night Grayson died, while he was walking his dog along the clifftop.'

'Do you think he'll tell?'

'I'll jolly well squeeze his scrawny neck until he does. It's time he came clean.'

'Have a good evening, ladies,' the barman called to them as they passed from the restaurant to the lobby. 'How did you find the cocktails?'

Effie lit up with admiration. 'Absolutely top hole, Robson. We tried to guess what was in them.'

Robson grinned smugly. 'And?'

'My analysis,' Dorothy replied, and reeled off what she thought was in the drinks.

'I'm impressed,' Robson nodded his head. 'Right on all but one. Not orange bitters – Cointreau. Well done.'

'Shall we have them as our regular evening aperitif in future, do you think, Effie?'

'Why not, and I must say that was good detecting analysis, Dorothy.'

The Man at the Walpole Bay Hotel

'I was thinking over dinner,' Dorothy said as they left the Walpole Bay. 'We should go and look for Ratty this evening.'

'Isn't it a bit late?' Effie looked at her watch. 'It's coming up for nine thirty.'

'Precisely, and I know just where he's to be found at this hour: the King's Arms. It's on his circuit. He does it every night. He starts out at the George, then goes to the Crown, after that it's the Wellington Hotel, then the King's Arms. Did I tell you that dreadful Karl Marx man used to take rooms there?'

'At the King's Arms? No.'

'Well, he did; a regular visitor. Mind you he's now dead – and anyway even if he were not, the war would have put a stop to jollies like that.

'All that aside, Ratty calls in there around seven, where he'll have four or five pints. After that he'll finish up for a last glass at around ten o'clock at the Fayreness, before taking that deplorable dog of his for its walk along the clifftops.'

'Good Lord, the man must have insides like a pickle barrel.'

'He'll certainly be well preserved when he departs this world, no doubt about that.'

The landlord at the King's Arms shook his head. Not been in here yet; most unusual for Mr Bumstead; very particular man in his habits.'

'Maybe he lingered at the Wellington, Effie.'

The two women went the short distance to the Wellington Hotel. 'Not seen hair nor hide of him,

The Man at the Walpole Bay Hotel

missus,' the barman told her. The news was the same at the Crown, and at the George.

'That's odd,' Dorothy tutted. 'Not like Ratty – not like Ratty at all.'

'Perhaps we should go to the Fayreness Hotel,' Effie suggested. 'We can check on the clifftop at the same time. After all, the dog will need its walk.'

*

'That's strange.' Dorothy drew the Prince Henry to a halt in front of the hotel. 'Why are there no lights on in the bars?' She got out of the car and went to the main reception door where the only light in the building was showing. The door was locked. Through the glass she could see a clerk sitting at the desk, his head bent over a newspaper. She rapped firmly on one of the window panes. The clerk looked up and, seeing her, came out from behind the desk to open the door.

'What's going on?' Dorothy asked insistently. 'Why is everything shut up?'

'We're closed, madam. New regulations: all licensed establishments to close at ten. We got a message this morning from the licensing justices. On account of the war. Seems the government wants to stop people drinking too much, so as they can work longer hours in the munitions factories.'

'But that's idiotic,' Dorothy fairly exploded with indignation. 'There aren't any munitions factories in Margate for people to work in. It's all farms; cabbages, hops, and fruit for miles around here.'

The Man at the Walpole Bay Hotel

The clerk looked sheepishly at her. 'Nevertheless, that's the order – rules are rules, madam.'

'What is it?' Effie asked, joining the two at the door.

'This gentleman says they must now shut up shop by ten o'clock. New government rules till the war is over. Did you ever hear such nonsense?'

'What about Ratty? Has he seen him?'

'Do you know Mr Bumstead, young man? Have you seen him this evening?'

The clerk smiled obligingly. 'Of course, everyone knows Mr Bumstead, madam – but no, I haven't seen him this evening.'

'Look,' Effie tugged at Dorothy's elbow and pointed across the grass towards the cliff. 'That looks like Ratty.' With that she waved her arm and shouted 'Cooo-eee,' at the top of her voice. The figure in the landscape hesitated and looked in their direction.

'Where's his dog? Ratty!' Dorothy shouted and made off across the grass.

She arrived slightly out of breath. 'Ratty,' she said imperiously, 'where the deuce have you been … ?'

The man turned to face her – it was not Ratty. 'Oh, do excuse me,' she said hurriedly, 'I thought you were someone else. So sorry.'

'All seems a bit odd to me,' Dorothy remarked, as they drove back to Effie's house. 'I Wonder where he's got to.' She looked at her fob watch. 'It's too late to do anything more tonight. I'm for my bed.

The Man at the Walpole Bay Hotel

See you in the morning. We can pick up our search again then.'

*

It was not the usual morning at the Seagull Guest House. It seemed strangely quiet in the breakfast room.

'Changeover day,' Mrs Clacket announced as she put down the plate of kippers in front of Inspector Page. 'Most of them gorn 'ome early. Glad to see the back of them two what sat over there.' She pointed an accusing finger at the table where the two Irishmen had sat confronting toast and plates of porridge every morning since he had arrived there. They were pleasant enough but they had kept themselves to themselves and, beyond the niceties of morning greetings, had resisted any conversation when Page had tried to open one.

'Strange lot them two,' Mrs Clacket observed tersely. 'Wouldn't eat the kippers. Just porridge and toast, all the same, every morning. Wouldn't eat nothing else – just the porridge and toast. Very odd pair. Probably up to no good, I'd say.'

Page nodded but said nothing. He had learned early on in his stay at the Seagull to avoid getting into a conversation with Mrs Clacket. Once started it was impossible to get her to stop. She had a view on everything.

'Well, I'll leave you in peace to enjoy your breakfast,' she said when it became obvious he was not going to engage.

The Man at the Walpole Bay Hotel

Page pushed away the plate of kippers. It was, in his view, an unappetising fish; too many bones. He pulled a piece of toast from the rack and applied a thick layer of butter to it. He bit into it without enthusiasm and contemplated the lack of progress on the Grayson case. By now he would normally have built a solid structure of evidence and been close to an arrest. This case had proved difficult from the beginning: no clues, no witnesses, no obvious leads. It was not going well.

The morning walk to the police station went some way to revive him, so that his mood had lightened by the time he sat down at his desk. 'Morning Constable Godley, anything new in the book this morning?'

'Not really, sir.' Godley put down a cup of tea in front of his boss. 'We have had a call from over St Nicholas way. The landlord of the Bell phoned to say there was an abandoned motor sitting at the roadside just down the way from him. Been there since yesterday.'

'Abandoned motor? Can't see what that's got to do with us. Probably broken down. He should notify that new mob, that Automobile Association lot. That's more up their street than ours.'

'Well, sir, he says the door on the car was hanging open and there was a gent's silk cravat lying on the ground next to it. Apparently had a rather fancy gold and pearl pin in it. He thought it was all looking a bit suspicious.'

'Hmm, all right. Get the sergeant to send a constable over to take a look.'

'What sort of motor was it?'

'A Rolls Royce, sir.'

'Was it by Jove. Expensive motor that.'

'Yes, sir. Only one gent hereabouts has a Rolls Royce.'

'Oh, yes, who's that?'

'One Reginald Bumstead, sir. Known locally as Ratty Reggie. A bit of a jack-the-lad. Made a shilling or two in his time. Tries to play the gent these days.'

Page rumpled his face and screwed up his mouth. 'Hmm, well get someone else to deal with it; we need to concentrate on this Grayson case.'

Chapter 15

Double dealing

Lucinda Coates was at the end of her task. For three weeks she had done little except observe the oystercatchers, from Pegwell Bay to the point at North Foreland lighthouse, counting them, peering at them through field glasses, noting down their feeding habits. Occasionally she went as far afield as Broadstairs; though more often than not that was an excuse to visit the wonderful ice cream parlour, run by an Italian immigrant family.

She had also made surreptitious breaks to take afternoon walks along the beach or the clifftops with Harry Donovan. She had found herself being drawn to his company more and more over her stay, and now it was coming to an end she felt strange pangs of disappointment.

They had begun to build up the semblance of a relationship; yet just when she thought it might be going somewhere he stepped back from any indication of a commitment. He was a strange

The Man at the Walpole Bay Hotel

man. There was something slightly out of step about him. He was polite, caring and attentive – yet there was something not quite right. There was a shroud around him, a mist that she felt might cloak a hidden identity. She was sure he was not telling her everything; that he had secrets to keep.

'I'm worried about Harry, Aunt Dorothy. I haven't seen him for several days,' Lucinda looked diffidently into her cup of coffee. 'His personal belongings are still in his room – but no Harry. Have you heard anything?'

Her aunt tried to sidestep the conversation, not wanting to get drawn into the subject, knowing that what she had learned of Donovan might not be what Lucinda would want to hear. 'Not really. But tell me, how is your work with those birds progressing? Is it all done yet?'

'Yes, thank you. I am just drafting the conclusion – but what about Harry? What do you think?'

'Think? Well.' Dorothy half paused, not sure how much she ought to say.

'Well what?'

Dorothy put a reassuring hand on her niece's arm. 'Oh, I'm sure he's just fine. Maybe he's gone back to London for a few days. You shouldn't worry.'

'But I *do* worry, Aunt. I would not like to think that anything untoward has happened to him.'

Dorothy stretched her face with an awkward look. She hesitated for a moment. 'Lucy dear, I hope this doesn't mean that you are getting too fond of Harry.'

Lucinda said nothing. She didn't need to; her expression said it all.

'Ah,' Dorothy said. The awkward look was replaced by one of general concern. 'I'm not sure he may be the right sort of man for you. Do be mindful of your feelings. I should not like to see you upset.'

'So you do know something, Aunt. Please tell me.'

Dorothy took a deep breath. 'Lucy, he would not be a suitable match. He is not what he seems.'

Lucinda's face fell. 'How so?'

This, Dorothy knew, was not going to be easy and she braced herself, but she was saved at the eleventh hour as Effie waltzed into the dining room.

'Hello, Lucy my dear, how are we?' Effie stopped short, then took half a step back. She peered hard at the glum-looking young woman in front of her. 'You look a bit peaky, dear; something wrong?'

'It's Harry, Effie. I'm worried about him. I haven't seen him in days, and I just wonder if he is all right.'

'Oh, right as rain, dear. I've just seen him; down in the town. Ooh, coffee. I'd murder the Pope for a cup. Absolutely gasping.'

'Never mind patricide,' Dorothy said briskly. 'Or whatever it is in the case of holy persons and clerics – what's all this about Harry?'

The Man at the Walpole Bay Hotel

Effie cast a cautious glance about her as if preparing to impart something highly sensitive. 'Two things actually – but they may be connected.'

Effie drew up a seat to their table and waved at a waiter. 'Can we have some coffee here do you think, please Herbert? Yes, Harry. I'd been to do a little shopping in the market – it's Freida's day off, you see – and lo and behold, there he was. I all but ran into him. He said to give you his greetings, my dear. He was off to the police station.' She nodded and smiled at Lucinda.

Lucinda immediately perked up. 'The police station!'

'Yes, he's still on bail, you know. That rather silly Inspector still has him marked as a suspect in the Grayson case.'

'I must go and see him,' Lucinda said, and hurriedly got up from the table. 'Do please excuse me, Aunt. You too, Effie.'

Dorothy raised an eyebrow. 'Poor Lucy, she really has been rather taken by that young man.'

'It does seem that way. I suppose it could complicate matters. You haven't let on about him have you?'

'Good gracious, no. Young women in love are not to be relied upon for discretion.'

'I suppose so.'

'Beyond doubt, dear girl. I recall my first heart flutter – I was twittering away like a dizzy skylark. No, it would not be good for Lucy to be told about Harry's true identity – nor his involvement with Seymour Trevelyan. It would serve no one.'

The Man at the Walpole Bay Hotel

'Excellent, here's the coffee,' Effie enthused, as a silver pot and a fresh cup were placed in front of her.

'So, tell me about meeting Harry? Did he have anything to say for himself?'

'No, not really. Just about his bail. There is one other thing. I didn't want to say it with Lucy present, but I followed him to the police station – discreetly, of course.'

'Naturally, I would expect nothing less than circumspection from you, Effie ... and?'

'And who should be loitering by the police station, waiting for him? Seymour Trevelyan. They immediately got into a huddle – and I must say, it looked very conspiratorial.'

'So, they are both back from London?'

'Yes, but there is more – the bit I particularly didn't want to say in Lucy's presence.'

Dorothy drew closer. 'Go on.'

'When I got home, I found Freida there.'

'Didn't you say it was her day off?'

'Precisely, so I was surprised – but doubly so when she told me what had transpired. She had forgotten her purse when she left that morning, you see. It was shortly after I had left, so the house was empty, except for cook. When Freida arrived she was surprised to find a man skulking round the side of the house. As soon as he saw her he made off in a hurry, pushing past her quite rudely. When she went inside she found cook all in a tizzy.'

Dorothy frowned. 'Whatever had happened?'

'Well, you see, cook had gone into the garden to cut some sage. The vegetable patch is right at the

The Man at the Walpole Bay Hotel

bottom of the garden. When she returned she says she heard someone in the study. Knowing the house should be empty, she armed herself with a stout rolling pin and went to investigate.'

'Good Lord, Effie, not intruders?'

'Just the one. When he saw cook he pushed her aside and ran out through the kitchen. That seems to be when Freida encountered him.'

'One of the Fenians?'

'Well, no. It seems not. From the description of both cook and Freida, I'd say it was uncomfortably like Harry. That's why I didn't want to say anything about it in front of Lucy. He was clearly after those German papers – or why else would he be there?'

'Aha! Effie, I get the sense that there are storm clouds gathering. We have to find Ratty.'

*

In the hall of Effie's house the telephone jangled out an insistent *tring, tring*.

The maid, Freida, picked up the earpiece. 'Good morning, the Dalrymple residence,' she said stiffly, then relaxed when she heard Dorothy's voice. 'Of course, Mrs Coates, I'll inform her right away. Dorothy hung on, the receiver pressed hard against her ear.

'Effie, sorry to interrupt your breakfast, but something has happened to Ratty. His motor has been found abandoned close by that barn – the one at St Nicks. I'll come over right away. We need to go and investigate. Dress in something practical –

oh, and Effie, I think it might be prudent to bring the Mauser with you. Just in case.'

*

'Why do you suppose Harry went to London?' Effie shouted over the rush of wind and the raucous growl of the Prince Henry's exhaust.

'I'm not sure,' Dorothy yelled back. 'Maybe he knew about whatever it is was that would happen to Ratty.'

There was no sign of Ratty's motor as they drove into the village. 'Gone,' Dorothy remarked as they passed the spot where it had been left.

'Maybe Ratty came back for it,' Effie speculated. 'Perhaps we've come on a wild goose chase.'

Dorothy drove as far as the Bell public house and pulled to a halt in front of it. 'We can make enquiries here. They reported it so they should know what's happened.'

Effie got our of the car and pressed her face up against a window. 'It seems to be closed. Should we knock, do you think?'

'We should.' Dorothy concurred and rapped vigorously on the front door. After a while there was the sound of someone drawing the bolts. A decrepit-looking cellar man stuck his head out.

'The motor's parked round the back in one of the stables,' he told them when they enquired about it. 'Keeping it there till the owner can be found. Constables suspect a bit of jiggery pokery gorn on.'

The Man at the Walpole Bay Hotel

'And which constables are those? Margate?'

'No, missus, they's from Canterbury.' He sniffed hard, wiped his nose with the back of his hand and ran it down his leather apron. 'Too serious I reckon fer Margate.'

'Thank you then.' Dorothy took a silver sixpence from her purse. 'Here, for you trouble, most obliged.'

The cellarman spat on the coin for good luck, rubbed it with his fingers and buried it in the pocket of his breeches.

'What now?' Effie said. 'Canterbury lockup? It might help to know what they've discovered.'

'I think so, but first we should take another look in that barn. After all, that is close to where the motor was found. He may have been there. It might yield some clues.'

They did not bother to make any effort to conceal their progress towards the barn. It was bright sunlight and there was no hiding their presence. Instead, they strode up the main track, Dorothy leading the way, with Effie following close behind. If seen, they would easily be mistaken for two ladies on an afternoon stroll; possibly in search of a suitable picnic spot, particularly since Effie was carrying a large soft bag in one hand.

'Why are you lugging that great big bag with you, Effie?' Dorothy said, looking questioningly at the ornate brocaded object that hung off two plaited handles. 'We're not going shopping, you know. What do you have in it?'

'The Mauser, of course,' Effie said quite earnestly. 'I have to put it somewhere. I simply can't wander around toting it openly. What would people say if I did that? They'd think I was some kind of hooligan.'

'Wouldn't it fit into a reticule?'

'Oh no, it's quite a bulky thing, you know – and I have two spare ammunition magazines, just in case.'

Dorothy's shoulders dropped in a gesture of resignation. 'Could you not have found something smaller?'

'I'm afraid it's the only gun Max had,' Effie said ruefully. 'Other than his hunting rifle, that is – and we left that back in Germany. Anyway, this is much more useful than one of those silly lady's handbag pistols. If you put it on fully automatic you can fire off the whole magazine; it's a sort of sub-machine gun really.'

'Good Lord, Effie, we're not going off to fight the war, you know.'

'Sorry, Dorothy.'

At that Dorothy laughed. 'Never mind, it's a comfort to know we can deal with a whole regiment of ruffians if necessary.'

They arrived at the barn and went straight to the main doors; a pair of heavy wood-planked leaves on iron hinges.

'Locked,' Dorothy announced, examining a substantial padlock. 'We'll have to go in the way we did before; remove those two planks from the back again.'

The Man at the Walpole Bay Hotel

Dorothy got her fingers through the gap between the boards and pulled. 'Drat, I should have brought that jemmy with us. It won't budge.' She stood back and thought for a moment, then bent down low enough to squint through the gap. 'That Model T has gone,' she half whispered over her shoulder to Effie. She took another look, peering in until her eyes became fully accustomed to the gloom. 'Oh my godfather's,' she said all panicky. 'Oh, the good Lord save us.' She straightened up abruptly.

Effie looked shocked by the outburst. 'Whatever is it?'

'It's Ratty. It seems they've done for him! They've hung him!'

'No!'

'Yes, he's dangling off the end of a rope in the rafters.'

'Oh dear, poor man. What shall we do?'

'We have to get in there – somehow. Search around in the grass, maybe we can find an abandoned stake or an old tool to lever that lock off.'

'Of course,' Effie nodded, 'but I could always shoot it off, you know – that might be quicker.'

Dorothy stopped what she was doing. 'Can you do that?' she asked.

'Oh, yes. I've done it before. It's quite easy, you know.'

'Then let us do that.'

Effie stood a yard back from the barn doors. 'You need to stand away,' she warned Dorothy.

'There's the risk of a ricochet, and there's bound to be splinters flying about.'

It took only one shot. A single '*crack!*'

It was quieter than Dorothy had anticipated, but nonetheless she cast about her furtively, wondering if the sound had alerted some curiosity. It had not. She pulled away what was left of the mangled padlock, which had now sprung open. They both hauled on one of the great doors. The hinges groaned in protest as they swung it outward.

Inside, the air was still and cool. The perfume of straw and the warm wood of the roof timbers, which had taken the morning sun, met their noses. They waited for a moment, allowing time for their eyes to adjust to the gloom. There in the middle, dangling off a short stout rope, was the body of Ratty; a rough hessian sack pulled over his head. There was a creak of rope binding on timber as it moved gently in the rush of the air they had caused by opening the door to the barn.

The two of them stood there, staring and motionless. The Model T truck had gone, and with it the crates of guns and ammunition.

'Are you sure that's Ratty?' Effie said, lowering her voice, as if she needed to show respect in the presence of the dead.

'Oh, without a doubt. I'd recognise that paunchy body anywhere.'

'How do we get him down?'

Dorothy gave a little shake of her head. 'We don't; we call the constables. It's their job.'

The Man at the Walpole Bay Hotel

'Well, at least let us remove that sack from his head. It's so undignified. He looks like a condemned man on the gibbet at Newgate.'

Dorothy considered the prospect for a moment. 'Very well, but how?' She walked a few paces to where a loft ladder was propped against a beam. 'That should do the trick. Will you do it or shall I? I'm used to looking the dead in the eye if you're squeamish.'

'Good Lord, no,' Effie whispered, 'the dead are dead – and that's it. A corpse doesn't bite you know.'

'Very well,' Dorothy said, dragging the ladder to where Ratty was suspended. 'I'll hold the ladder, you shin up and take the hood off. Right, up you go.'

Effie went up, a rung at a time, moving easily to the top. 'Well, if that isn't the giddy limit,' she called down when she got to the body. 'They've hung him up by his belt and braces.' Deftly she turned the body towards her, then pulled off the hood. 'Oh poor man,' she gasped. 'They left him with no dignity even in death. Look, they've jammed an old sock in his mouth and tied it with a gag. It seems they might have suffocated him first, then hung him up.'

'Well, that's of no consequence now,' Dorothy said, 'you've restored his dignity, now come down.'

'Goodbye old Ratty,' Effie said, and gave the corpse a gentle pat on the cheek.

The corpse opened one eye and winked at her.

'Aahhh!' Effie shrieked and struggled not to fall of the ladder. 'Oh my God, it winked at me!'

'*What*!'

'Ratty, he winked at me'.

'He's alive?'

'I think he is.'

'Well, take the sock out his mouth and ask him; for *goodness* sakes, Effie.'

Effie untied the gag and as she pulled it away there was an explosive '*pewtt*' as Ratty spat out the sock. 'I knew you'd be comin,' he said, in a voice as crusty as an old pie. 'Just didn't know you was gonna to take yer time. What kept yer?'

Dorothy was now standing with her arms folded, something approaching a scowl on her face. 'Well, a modicum of gratitude would not go amiss, Ratty. Now, how are we going to get you down without you breaking a leg. They did a pretty good job. You're bound up like a Sunday chicken. What we need is a knife to cut through those bonds.'

'In my bag, there's a clasp knife,' Effie called down.

'They got away, them miserable double crossers,' Ratty growled when he was at last freed from his bonds.

'The Fenians?'

'Who else? Took my money, they did. Took the guns too, and legged it.'

'Where are they going, Ratty, do you know?'

'Bristol, Mrs Coates. I 'erd how there were a boat there – waiting fer 'em.'

'That'll be the *Regina Maris*, for certain,' Effie chimed in.

'I'm sure you're right,' Dorothy said. 'How long have they been gone, Ratty?'

'They left this morning. I 'erd 'em discussing how they was taking a cross country route so as to avoid the constables; out through Sussex and Dorset. That's what they were talking of.'

Dorothy gave the matter a few moments thought. 'We need a plan of campaign,' she decided, 'and I don't know about you, Effie dear, but I'm gasping for a cup of tea. I saw there was a tearoom at that store in the village. We should go there and lay out our *modus operandi*. You'd better come along too, Ratty – and don't look so sour. I shan't ask you to drink tea.'

'Would you order the tea?' Dorothy asked Effie. 'I'll get that very useful Automobile Association gazetteer. It's in the Prince Henry, shan't be a jiffy.'

When she came back, Dorothy unfolded the map at the back of the gazetteer. 'What time did they leave, Ratty?'

'Around two hours ago, missus.'

'In that Ford truck?'

'That's it.'

'It'll take all day and half the night in that jalopy. Now let's see. What time is it, Effie? I left my watch at home.'

'Just gone eleven.'

'Flat out and empty that Model T might manage forty miles an hour. The Prince Henry can do twice that speed, and a bit more for good measure. And the truck is loaded, so – probably not much more than thirty at its best.'

Ratty nodded agreement. 'But the road most likely ain't good and them guns weighs. So bit slower I'd say, missus.'

'In which case, allowing for holdups at junctions, villages, the occasional horse and cart – they've probably covered around forty miles already.'

Effie stared down at the map. 'Do you think we can catch them, then?'

Dorothy ran her finger along the route, mentally adding the distances indicated between the towns. 'Tunbridge Wells.' She tapped a finger on the town name. 'That's where we'll catch up with them, and we shan't even have to go flat out.'

'Well, let us thank the Lord for that,' Effie sighed with relief. 'I have to say, I did not relish the idea of charging recklessly through the countryside flat out.'

'Don't fret, dear girl. That truck is no match for the Prince Henry. Ratty, get your Rolls Royce and come on after us. Best if you can bring your chauffeur too. We shall need all hands to the pumps on this one.'

Ratty frowned and screwed up his mouth. 'So how does this work then, missus?'

'I estimate we'll bag them somewhere on the road. There's a public house in Tunbridge Wells called the White Horse. Meet us there.'

Ratty gave the women a cautious look. 'Now wait a minute, missus. You be careful. Them are

The Man at the Walpole Bay Hotel

dangerous characters you're dealing with. Revolutionaries them Fenians. They'll do fer ya. Both of ya – if you get in their way.'

'Not with Annie Oakley here, they won't. Now off you go Ratty, there's a good chap. We shall see you at the White Horse. Oh, and on second thoughts, why don't you bring your man along as well. I've heard he's quite useful if it should come to fisticuffs.'

*

The Prince Henry slowed as they came to the outskirts of the small town of Ashford. The noise of their progress lessened to a gentle purr from the engine and a happy gurgle from the exhaust. Normal speech became possible once more. 'How are we doing, Effie?'

'It's taken us forty-nine minutes so far. Pretty good going. At this rate we should be on them within the hour. By the bye, what did you mean when you referred to me as Annie somebody or other, to Ratty?'

'Oakley,' Dorothy said firmly, 'don't you remember? The American sharpshooter. She came for the old Queen's Jubilee – that American, the frontiersman, Buffalo Bill and his Wild West show. I went to see it with George. Rough riders and Indians. Very stirring stuff.'

'Yes, of course, now you mention it. Didn't she used to shoot at a target with the rifle over her shoulder whilst looking in a mirror.'

'She did, and a bullseye every time.'

'I suppose I *could* be mistaken for that woman; if I were standing with my back to you.'

'You could.'

'Funny thing really.'

'What's that?'

'How easily we can be fooled about someone when we can't see their face. Max used to say that was the only way we really knew someone.'

'I suppose so.'

'Yes, once I embarrassed myself in the Tiergarten. I had arranged to meet Max. When I saw him standing there in his usual hat and morning coat, admiring the ducks on the lake, I crept up behind him and knocked his hat off his head. I wanted to surprise him, you see.'

'Well I'm sure you did.'

'Yes – except it wasn't Max. It was a complete stranger. I was *so* embarrassed. When I told Max he laughed and said that was a common mistake; many people look the same from behind, and that we can only really tell someone by looking at their face.'

Dorothy went quiet for a moment, then she stood on the brakes and brought the Prince Henry to a skidding halt. 'Good Lord, Effie, *that's it*! I think you just solved the Grayson case.' Dorothy started the car moving again. 'We need to find a telephone kiosk. I have to make a call.'

'Who too?'

'Mrs Muggeridge. I'll tell you later. First we have to catch up with those Fenians.'

*

The Man at the Walpole Bay Hotel

There were a lot of new faces at breakfast in the dining room of the Seagull Guest House. Page looked over to the table where the two Dublin men had sat. Businessmen, he had concluded. They had stayed longer than the fortnight holiday makers, and largely kept themselves to themselves. He had tried to make casual conversation with them but they had always seemed reluctant to engage.

'Irish,' Mrs Clacket said pejoratively. 'Strange lot the Irish. Like foreigners but not – if you catch my meaning.'

Page raised an eyebrow. 'No, I don't think I do. How do you mean, Mrs Clacket?'

'*Like Americans*,' she exclaimed, indignant that Page had not immediately concurred. 'You know; speak our language, well sort of, but they're not us, are they? They're more, mmm, foreigners. Funny foreign 'abits and all that.'

'Oh, I see what you mean. Well, yes, I suppose they are a bit different.'

'Suspicious, I'd say.'

'Well, I wouldn't go as far as that, Mrs Clacket.'

'Su-spic-ious, Inspector.' She wagged a finger to underline the statement. 'Any man who doesn't want a kipper for his breakfast is *definitely* suspicious. There's a war on, Inspector. Spies are abroad, Mr Asquith says so and he should know, he's the prime minister. Exotic oriental women. You need to be careful of them now.'

Page drew a deep breath and stood up. 'I don't think there's too much danger of oriental temptresses in the Seagull, Mrs Clacket. I must be off. I bid you a good day.'

When Page arrived at the police station he was confronted by a more than usually upbeat Constable Godley.

'I've had a note from that Mrs Coates, sir. Hand-delivered this morning by the housekeeper, Mrs Muggeridge.'

'Oh yes, and what does it say, lad?'

'A bit strange really, sir. She says she wants to meet with you this evening at the Walpole Bay Hotel; that she has solved the Grayson murder.'

Page's face fell. He made a huffing noise and shook his head from side to side, tutting dismissively. If it wasn't Mrs Clacket and spies, it was these two ladies.

'Margate, Godley, is a town full of women who want to tell me how to do my job.'

'There is one other thing, sir.'

'Go on.'

'Scotland Yard called, first thing. Their forensics have found blood stains at the Kensington house where we know Donovan has been staying. The blood is a match for the dead German, Ernst Weber – and I sent the Yard the new prints we took from Donovan the other day, when he came back from the dead, so to speak. Turns out his dabs are all over the furniture in the same room.'

Page's face glowed with triumph. 'That's it then; we've got him bang to rights. If he murdered Weber, then why not Grayson and that other cove. I'm not sure why the others but I am pretty certain he will now come clean. And if he won't tell, I'm sure his accomplice, Mr Seymour Trevelyan, will be happy to spill the beans when we threaten to charge him with accessory to murder.'

Page clapped his hands together and wrung them energetically.

'Well done, Godley. I think this calls for a cuppa.'

Chapter 16

The showdown

Barely ten minutes after they had left Ashford the road degenerated. There was a jarring thump as they came off the bitumen and hit the rough stony surface. It had been graded and rolled but to not much effect. The surface was rippled like a washboard. The Prince Henry slowed. Dorothy muttered a barely disguised oath; words of the sort ladies were not supposed to utter.

'Do you think we can still catch them at this pace?' Effie shouted above the sound of shingle rattling up under the chassis and wings.

'If we slow, then they'll have to as well,' Dorothy called back. 'Probably more so because of the weight of the load they are carrying. So the advantage is with us. Just hold on tight, I'm going to crack on.'

'Well, I hope there won't be a lot more like this; the dust is ruining my make-up. My eyes will be as red as a clown's nose if this carries on for much longer.'

'Goggles!' Dorothy yelled, pointing at the cubby hole in the dashboard. 'In there – and hold a handkerchief over your nose.'

Another jarring thump announced that they had jumped back onto the bitumen again. The rattling of stones stopped and everything felt very smooth and quiet.

'Well, thank the Pope for that,' Effie said, pulling the handkerchief away from her mouth.

'Save the plaudits for later, dear girl, this won't last for long. Look there,' Dorothy gestured ahead of them. 'See the dust plume? That'll be them, I'll wager a good half-crown on it.'

With another soul-jarring bump they crashed off the ridge that marked the end of the sealed road and dropped several inches onto another unmade stretch. The staccato rattling came back once more, together with a fine plume of grey dust and a rib-rattling vibration. As they closed on the vehicle in front they could make out the shrouded image that was unmistakably the Model T.

'I'll try to get past them,' Dorothy shouted. 'Keep the Mauser handy. If Ratty is right things might become nasty.'

Dorothy pulled the Prince Henry out from behind the truck and put her foot hard down. The car leapt forward, bucking like a wild stallion. The driver in the Model T swerved wildly sideways, trying to prevent them getting past. Dorothy heaved the Prince Henry away to avoid a collision.

The Man at the Walpole Bay Hotel

There was a deafening bang and the car lurched uncontrollably in a long broadside slew. Effie squealed; Dorothy shouted something unmentionable. The Prince Henry snaked as Dorothy fought with the wheel. They lost speed and limped to a stop.

'Damnation, Effie, they've got away.'

Effie had her hand clenched around the grab handle on the dashboard, her knuckles white with the pressure. 'Did they hit us? What happened? I thought I heard a gunshot.'

'I don't think so, I'll take a look. It could have been a sideswipe,' Dorothy said, getting out of the Prince Henry.

'Well, what is it?' Effie was now out of the car as well and dusting down her clothes. 'What a *mess* this dust has made of my dress. I'm covered in it.'

Dorothy was standing at the back of the Prince Henry staring down at the rear wheel. 'It wasn't a gunshot, Effie, and they didn't hit us either. Look. A blowout. What rotten luck. We nearly had them there.' She kicked at the shredded tyre with the toe of her Chelsea boot. 'Good job it was a back tyre and not a front, or we'd have probably done a somersault and come a cropper.'

Effie sniffed. 'What now?'

'We'll have to change the wheel. Put on the spare.'

'Can you do that?'

'*Of course*,' Dorothy said assertively. 'That nice salesman at the Vauxhall garage showed me how. Come on, lend a hand. It's quite simple really.'

The road improved again and they settled down to a decent speed as Dorothy pushed the Prince Henry as fast as she dared. Even so, it was another half hour before they sighted the Model T again. It had stopped in the car park of a roadside tearoom, half hidden behind two larger trucks.

'There,' Dorothy shouted as they sailed past the place. A hundred yards further on she pulled to a halt.

'That was them all right,' Effie said. 'What do you think we should do?'

Dorothy tightened her mouth and rumpled her nose. 'It'll be tricky, but we have to apprehend them.'

'What do you suggest?'

'A stick-up, of course. We've got the Mauser. They won't be expecting us. We just say hands up, and then tie them up. I've brought some cord along just for this eventuality.'

Effie looked uncertain at that. 'What if we say hands up – and they don't.'

'Well, then you have to shoot them.'

'Oh, I'm not certain about that. I don't want to end up on the gallows.'

'No, no, you don't shoot to kill, Effie. Just shoot them somewhere that's not vital but a bit painful. Like you did with that seafarer fellow who was threatening to do for us back in the old folly at Botany Bay. You could do that, couldn't you?'

Effie thought about it for a moment then nodded. 'I suppose in the foot might do the trick.'

The Man at the Walpole Bay Hotel

'Right, we know what the plan is. Let's go back and lie in wait for them. I'll just turn the Prince Henry around.'

'Oh golly, I don't think you need bother, Dorothy.' Effie stood transfixed as the Model T came towards them.

The truck pulled up alongside them, blocking them in so there was no escape. Two men got out. 'Well, well, Tommy boy. Do you see what we have here?'

'I do, Danny, I do.'

'Snoopers, I'd say.'

'I think that's right.'

'I think you must be mistaken, gentlemen,' Dorothy said, urgently trying to find a way out of the problem.

'No, no,' the one called Tommy said, shaking his head and raising his eyebrows in a mocking fashion. 'The only mistake here is yours. You see, we are definitely *not* gentlemen.' He swung a hand in an open slap to the side of Dorothy's head, sending her crashing against the Prince Henry. She lost her footing and fell. Effie let out a shrill cry. 'You ruffian! Keep your hands off her!'

'Aw, shut yer gob, or I'll shut it for ya. We know who you are and what you're up to. Spies and snoopers. Well, we know how to deal with them. Jacko! Come out here. There's work to be done.'

There was movement in the back of the truck. The tarpaulin peeled back and a large rough-looking man climbed out from under the cover. Dorothy had struggled to her feet, her hand to her face rubbing the spot where a dark bruise was forming. A trickle of blood ran down from one corner of her mouth. Effie put an arm around her. 'We know what your game is,' Dorothy said angrily, 'and you won't get away with it. The police know where we are and they will be on their way here right now.'

All three men broke into an ugly laugh. 'Forget it, lady,' the one called Danny grinned. 'You'll be long done for by the time anyone finds you. Jacko here will see to that.'

Dorothy moved closer to Effie. 'The Mauser,' she whispered.

'In my handbag. In the back of the car.'

Dorothy's face fell. 'Good grief, Effie, it's no good there.'

'Sorry.'

'We have to see if we can get to it – it's our only chance.'

Effie turned to confront the three men. 'I need to get my handbag. My friend needs something to stop her face bleeding.' She took a step towards the Prince Henry.

'The hell she does,' Tommy grunted, and hauled Effie back by the shoulder. She cursed at him and he responded with a hard punch to her midriff, causing her to vomit. She bent double, choking and spitting. Suddenly things were going badly wrong. What had seemed like a good adventure was now turning sour.

'Danny, we need to get out of here,' Tommy said. 'Maybe these old biddies are telling it straight about the cops. We can't hang around.'

The Man at the Walpole Bay Hotel

Danny looked at the two woman and shook his head. 'Jacko, take care of them. And when you have, follow on after us. Shouldn't take you long in this fine machine,' he said, pointing at the Prince Henry.

'Come along now, ladies.' The man who had crawled out from the back of the truck grinned. He spoke with a strong American accent; his voice joking and charged with a false sympathy that gave it a sinister edge.

The two women stood helpless and watched as Danny and Tommy got back into the cab of the Model T, started the engine, and drove away. After it had gone from their sight, and a quiet had settled on the road, the American pulled a pistol from his jacket. 'Okay, we're going for a ride. You ... ,' he prodded Dorothy with the muzzle of the gun, 'you drive, lady.' He turned to Effie. 'You, get in next to her. Okay. I'm in the back behind you.' He glared at Dorothy. 'Try any stunts and your friend here gets it. Right, lady, put your foot on the gas and let's get outa here.'

'Where to?' Dorothy asked, trying to recover her composure.

'Just go straight down the road. I'll tell ya when to stop.'

'Sorry,' she said, turning her head to Effie. 'I didn't mean for it to turn out like this.'

Effie put a hand on her friend's arm and squeezed it. 'That's all right; it wasn't your fault.' Seconds later, she burst into floods of tears. Her chest heaved and her sobs of anguish grew louder and louder until she was finally bawling like a destressed child.

Jacko got agitated, then angry. 'For crying out loud will ya *shut* the hell up.'

Effie turned in the seat, still snivelling. 'I need my handbag, I need a hanky,' she whined. 'It's there. Give it to me.'

Jacko picked it off the seat and heaved it across into her lap. 'Here, I hope it helps,' he growled.

Effie smiled, 'Oh it does.'

'Good. Now stow it.' He poked Dorothy hard in the shoulder. 'Right, this is the end of the line. Pull over here.'

The place where they stopped was by a wooded coppice of tangled hazel trees. They got out of the car and stood waiting, anxious looks on their faces.

'In there,' Jacko said. He pushed the gun back into his pocket and began to herd them in the direction of the thicket. They struggled through until they emerged into a small clearing. 'Okay this'll do. Real sorry about this,' he said, but the smirk on his face made a lie of the apology.

'Oh, don't be, there is really no need,' Effie said, and delving into her copious handbag pulled out the Mauser, in the same moment sliding back the breech and pointing it at him. 'Now,' she said, 'keep your hands where I can see them.'

There was a moment of silence as a look of disbelief spread across Jacko's face. Then he burst into a raucous laugh. 'Give over lady, you ain't gonna shoot me. I bet you don't even know how that thing operates.'

The Man at the Walpole Bay Hotel

'Oh, she will, I assure you,' Dorothy insisted, 'and she certainly knows how.'

Jacko looked from one to the other of them. 'You're kidding me.'

He grinned and took a step forward. There was a sharp crack. Jacko stared in disbelief, then let out a roar of pain. He went to lunge at Effie but his leg gave way and he fell. 'You *bitch*! You *bitch*! You *rotten bitch. Jesus, you shot me.*' He grasped at his right foot, squeezing his fingers over a hole in the toe of his shoe out of which blood was oozing.

'Well, I did warn you she would,' Dorothy grinned with satisfaction. 'Now stop moaning. I'm going to tie your hands behind your back, then we'll get your shoe off and take a look at that foot.'

'*Jesus Christ! That hurts.*'

'Yes, well, I'm afraid it would,' Effie said patronisingly. 'Now do stop whining – it's only a toe.'

'Yes, for goodness sake pull yourself together, man, and stop snivelling,' Dorothy admonished. 'I saw men suffer *far* worse injuries when George was posted to the Khyber Rifles.'

'Oh,' Effie said, pulling the shoe off the injured foot, 'that must have been awful; billeted up there on the Afghan frontier. Was the accommodation any good?'

'*Holy God*!' Jacko yelled. 'Willya watch what you're doing. That damn well hurt.'

'Primitive,' Dorothy said, ignoring the shouts from Jacko. 'But the officer's mess was halfway decent, and the countryside quite breathtaking.

The Man at the Walpole Bay Hotel

Mind you, fighting those Pathan tribesmen during the revolts was pretty sticky. Some jolly awful wounds George had to patch up – though the patients didn't make half the fuss this one's kicking up.' She scowled at Jacko.

'We shall need something to disinfect this wound,' Effie said pulling away the blood-soaked sock. 'Do you have anything in the Prince Henry we might use?'

'Meths, and there's some lint. I use it to clean my hands if I have to get under the bonnet and tinker. Just a jiffy and I'll get it.'

'I think we should get rid of this too,' Effie said, delving into Jacko's coat pocket and pulling out the automatic pistol he was carrying. 'You won't need this where you're going.' She threw it a few feet away into the undergrowth. 'There, now that's better.'

When Dorothy came back it was without the meths, and she was not alone. Behind her the two Fenians, Danny and Tommy, pushed her roughly through the undergrowth, shoving her along and prodding her in the back with a short wooden club. 'Don't try anything, missus,' Danny growled as they came into the clearing, 'or your friend here gets her skull cracked. Jacko, what the devil's gone on here!?'

'They had a gun,' Jacko pointed accusingly at Effie. 'The *bitch* shot me – in the foot.'

'Did she now?' Danny grinned. 'I'd say that wasn't a nice thing to do, missus.'

Tommy began laughing.

The Man at the Walpole Bay Hotel

Effie made a grab for her bag and the Mauser. It was only a step away from her but Tommy got to it first. He stamped a foot on the bag and grabbed Effie by her outstretched arm. He yanked her away and flung her sideways with no more effort than if she had been a rag doll.

Danny pushed Dorothy over to where Effie was struggling back onto her feet. He grinned at Jacko and gave a short laugh. 'Fancy now, two genteel ladies getting the drop on a great big fellah like yerself. That's a story to tell in the local shebeen if ever there was one.'

'Just *shut* the hell up, will ya,' Jacko snarled. 'Gimme a hand up. I'm gonna do for these two cows right now.' Between them they pulled Jacko upright. He grunted, shuffled painfully over to Effie and with his shoe raised in his hand, hit her hard across the side of her face. Effie gasped out a sigh and fell like a stone to the ground.

'I say we do for them now,' Jacko snapped, and spat angrily down onto Effie's sprawled body.

'No, you go back to the truck,' Danny said, jerking his head at Jacko. 'Go on now, before you pass out. You've lost I don't know how much blood. Tommy, you go with him. I'll settle it for these two.' He watched as Jacko lurched off in the direction of the road, one arm clinging onto Tommy's shoulder.

'Right, my darlings,' he said grimly. 'Your turn now.' He stepped close to Dorothy and took a swing at her head with the club. Dorothy shied away awkwardly to one side. She lost her balance and toppled backwards, the club only managing a glancing blow to the side of her forehead. She landed heavily in the undergrowth. Danny moved in for the kill. In that moment he felt a hefty thump to the back of his leg. He turned angrily as Effie took a second kick at him. He threw out an arm, grabbing her by the shoulder and aiming to strike her with the club but she bit him hard in the wrist. He let go, at the same time knocking her sideways with the back of his hand. 'Holy Mary, yer fecking little harridan.' He put his wrist to his mouth momentarily as if to stop the blood. He quickly abandoned that idea and instead decided to finish the business with Dorothy. He turned, raised the club, and stopped.

Dorothy had struggled back onto her feet – and he was staring into the muzzle of Jacko's gun. 'Oh, *Mother of God!*' he blurted, dropped the club and ran weaving into the bushes. Dorothy closed her eyes and pulled the trigger. The bang was deafening and the kickback almost pulled the gun out of her hand. The shot went wide but it didn't matter – it had saved them. She vaguely heard a shout from the direction of the truck and then the sound of an engine kick into life. She stood there shivering for a moment, then she started to feel the pain in her head where the club had hit her. Effie came over to her, brushing herself down. For a few moments the two of them indulged a little hug.

'That was closer than I ever want things to get – ever,' Dorothy said.

Effie was nodding. 'I imagine that was Jacko's gun; where did you find it?'

The Man at the Walpole Bay Hotel

'It was there, in the bushes, where I fell. I couldn't believe my luck. It made an *awfully* loud bang – my ears are still whistling.'

'Well, it would do,' Effie said knowingly. 'It's a Colt 45. They're big noisy things. Not like my Mauser. Much more refined.'

'Would it have done much damage – if I'd hit him, that is?'

'Goodness yes. You'd have blown a great big hole in him. Just as well you missed. You're not a very good shot, are you. You were wide by a country mile. You could do with some practice, you know.'

Dorothy winced. 'I'd rather leave the shooting business to you, if you don't mind, thanks awfully. Where is your bag, by the way?'

'Over there. I suppose we should get going. Shall we chase after them?'

'No, Effie, I don't think we should. I know we now have two guns, but *they* have a whole truckload. I don't think we should consider getting into a shoot-out with them. It might end badly. Besides I have a better idea. Come on, let's get the Prince Henry. We have to meet up with Ratty at that hotel, and we can get a cocktail or two. Frankly I'm gasping.'

'Oh, no.' Dorothy groaned as they stood contemplating the empty road where the Prince Henry had been parked. 'The bounders, they've taken the car. Well, that almost beggars belief. It makes things *very* awkward.'

'It does a bit,' Effie agreed. 'What to do?'

The Man at the Walpole Bay Hotel

'I suppose we shall just have to walk. That tearoom is not far along the road from here. With a bit of luck they'll be connected to a telephone line and we can phone the hotel in Tunbridge Wells. If Ratty's there he can come out and rescue us.'

The woman behind the till at the tearoom looked apologetic. 'Sorry, ladies, no telephone here, I'm afraid.' She was a bit shocked as she looked at their injuries. 'You seem like you've had a bad time of it. Whatever happened?'

'Robbers,' Dorothy said. 'Held us up. Assaulted us and stole our motor car. Scoundrels.'

'Well, I never did. You poor souls. Such a dreadful thing to happen. You go out back, my dears. There's a ladies room where you can have a wash and brush-up. My husband is out at the moment, but when he gets back I'll have him run you over to Ashford. You can report it to the constables there.'

Fifteen minutes later both women returned looking refreshed, though Effie could not disguise a black eye and a bruise to the cheek. Dorothy, too, looked the worse for the ordeal; both her eyes were black, there was a yellowing lump on her forehead where she had been caught by the club, a livid welt on her cheek where she had received the slap in the face from one of the Fenians.

'How are you now?' the tearoom lady asked. 'Would you like some tea? You look as if you could do with it.'

The Man at the Walpole Bay Hotel

'Oh, how kind of you,' Effie said, her face folding up with a stab of pain as she tried to put on a smile. 'I don't suppose you have something a little stronger?'

'Well, we're not licensed, I'm afraid, but I dare say I could find something a little cheering in my kitchen pantry. I'll just take a look.'

'There,' she smiled, coming back into the room carrying a tray with a bottle and three glasses. 'It's only Madeira wine, I'm afraid. It's what I use to make the trifle. Will that do?'

'Yes, that'll more than do,' Effie affirmed enthusiastically. 'Wouldn't you say, Dorothy?'

'Oh, quite definitely.'

'I've brought three glasses. If you don't mind I'll join you. I'm Iris – so nice to meet you. I don't get a lot of female company out here, you see. It's mostly men; hauliers with their lads. Now, do tell me all about what happened. It's nice to have a little female company and some girl talk. Shall I pour?'

Effie and Dorothy both nodded.

Chapter 17

Revelation

In the comfortable back seat of his Rolls Royce, Ratty sat smoking a fat cigar and surveying the passing scenery. He was still stewing over the way he had been trussed up and double-crossed by the two Irishmen.

He had paid them well to arrange for a consignment of machine guns to be delivered to the port of Tangiers.

They had readily accepted his commission money, and a promise of payment for the merchandise on delivery. Then they had turned crooked on him; left him bound and gagged with little care as to his fate.

Up front, his man, Billy Arden, sat next to Higgs the chauffeur. Billy had been a prize fighter in London, but he'd hung up his gloves after an illegal fight; one in which his opponent got so soundly whipped he took a grudge about it to the local magistrate. Billy was fined and bound over

The Man at the Walpole Bay Hotel

never to fight again. The fine was more than Billy could raise and he faced the prospect of jail time. Ratty bailed him out and offered him the position of gentleman's gentleman. Having been batman to a general in the South African wars, Billy took to the post like a duck to a pond.

'Tearooms, boss,' Billy shouted through the glass partition. 'You wanna cuppa?' Higgs slowed the limousine and waited for the instruction.

'Nah, keep goin, I could do wiv a pint, not bloody tea, Billy. We'll get one at that White 'orse pub.'

Two miles beyond the tearoom, Higgs slowed the Rolls again. 'Looks like a motor broken down ahead, sir. Shall I stop to see if they require assistance?'

'Yeah, why not. You're a dab 'and wiv motors, Billy. See if you can fix it for 'em.'

'Looks like abandoned, guv,' Billy called back to his boss. 'Can't see no one around. Shall we motor on?'

'Yeah, why not.'

Higgs prepared to move but then Ratty changed his mind. 'Nah, 'ang abaht, 'ang abaht. I recognise that. There ain't a lot of them around. That's Mrs Coates's motor – money on it.'

Ratty opened the door and got out. 'That's a bit funny,' he said, as Billy joined him. 'No sign of the ladies. I 'ope they ain't got 'emselves into trouble. I did warn 'em.'

He looked around for a bit, then cupping his hands to his mouth shouted their names. There

The Man at the Walpole Bay Hotel

was no answer. He tried again. Billy Arden stuck his head inside the Prince Henry. 'Aye, aye, guv, look 'ere.'

'Whatcha got, Billy?'

'Blood, guv – all over the place.'

Ratty shook his head slowly. 'I did warn 'em not to mess wiv them lads. Don't look good, Billy. Best turn round. Gotta report this. Ashford's nearest. Take it away, Higgsy. I'll follow in Mrs Coates motor. Billy, you come wiv me.'

*

In the tearoom, the three ladies sat and talked; Dorothy unfolded the story of their encounter with the Fenians and Jacko.

'Thank you, Iris,' Dorothy said, as she sipped the last drop from her glass, the story now concluded. 'That was rather good Madeira; don't you agree? Effie.'

'Indeed. I could probably manage a second glass – if that is all right?'

The sound of a vehicle scrunched on the gravel and pulled up outside. 'Ah, that'll be my husband I should think.' Iris got up from the table and went to the window. 'Oh no, strangers. Customers, I dare say.' The door opened to the jingling of a bell, and three men walked in. They were not customers.

Dorothy jumped up. 'Ratty! My dear chap, am I pleased to see you. How did you know we were here?'

The Man at the Walpole Bay Hotel

'I didn't, missus. I come in ter find if they 'ad a telephone. We found your motor, a few miles up the road. There were a lot of blood. We was gonna call the coppers ...' Ratty stopped mid-sentence, '... oh my gawd, whatever 'appened to yer faces, fer crying out loud.'

'Later,' Dorothy insisted, 'it's a long story, Ratty. Right now we need to get to Ashford – there's a lot to be done.'

Ratty peered closely at Dorothy's face. One eye had almost closed over, and the other one looked like it might not be far behind. 'I reckon you're not fit to drive, Missus. Tell yer what. You and yer friend 'ere, go wiv Higgsy my chauffeur. Billy and me'll follow on in your motor. Wha'dya say?'

'Yes, I think you're right, but we need to be quick about it.'

'This is most luxurious,' Effie said, smoothing her hand across the moleskin upholstery in the back of the Rolls.

Dorothy settled herself down comfortably. 'I must say I thought we might really be done for back there – just for a moment.'

Effie wrinkled her nose, which was the nearest she could get to a smile with causing pain. 'Jolly exciting, though, wouldn't you say? Quite like the old days when I was out there in Mafeking. Bullets flying around, people getting shot, and all that sort of stuff.'

'Well, I think I could probably do with a little less excitement of that sort, if that's alright by you Effie.'

The Man at the Walpole Bay Hotel

*

In the Margate police station the pace was quickening and there was an air of expectancy. Inspector Page had spent the morning putting his case together. There was a half empty cup of tea sitting on his desk, which had long ago gone cold. DC Godley had been running back and forth since breakfast time. Papers had to be gathered and collated; facts marshalled and compiled into a coherent chronology.

'Evidence, Godley, evidence,' Page had announced the moment he had arrived in his office, and Godley had been despatched in every direction. The case had to be watertight if they were to take it before a magistrate. Now, by late afternoon, Page deemed the work done and he was satisfied he could carry the day.

'All right, lad,' he said when Godley had finally brought the last sheet of paper from the files, 'observe and learn. This is how we do it: carefully and methodically. Get yourself a seat next to me, lad.'

Godley pulled a chair round to Page's side of the desk and sat next to him.

'Now, what have we got? Principal suspect: Henry Charles Raleigh St George Donovan. Seriously, I ask you, where *do* these toffs get their names from?'

Godley sniggered.

The Man at the Walpole Bay Hotel

'Victim: Benedict Arthur Grayson.' Page nudged his constable with his elbow, 'Now that's what I call a regular name.'

Godley nodded agreement. 'Yes, sir.'

'Principal witness: the waiter at the Fayreness Hotel. He identified Donovan as holding a conversation with Grayson around eleven o'clock on the night Grayson died. They were both seen leaving the saloon bar at around the same time. The pathologist puts the time of death at around eleven to eleven thirty. *So*, there we have our man.'

'Definitely suspicious, sir.'

'More than suspicious, Godley. These are facts. They are substantiated. There are witnesses, and a pathology report. Can't really be challenged.'

'Motive: that's a bit more tricky. There is no obvious motive. However – we cannot rule out that Grayson possibly stumbled on something, saw something, or knew something.'

Page paused and stretched out his arms; stiff from sitting at the desk all day.

'Now we come to the circumstantial evidence. Not sufficient on its own, but standing alongside the proven facts it plays a strong supporting role.

'One: Donovan has been observed on several occasions, hanging about the clifftops close to where Grayson went over; there are witnesses.'

'Mrs Coates and her friend,' Godley affirmed.

'And the niece, Lucinda. She saw him together with Trevelyan up there on at least two occasions.'

'Probably reccying the site of the crime, sir.'

'Exactly. Point number two: Donovan is known to use an address in Kensington. The same address in which the German, Ernst Weber, was seen just prior to his death. Positive ID by the cleaning lady.'

'Another good witness.'

'Precisely so. Then, Weber's body is found washed up at Gravesend, a bit of rope round his neck. A matching piece of rope was found tied off to the parapet rail on Blackfriars Bridge. Supposed suicide – except that Weber's blood was found all over the carpet of an upstairs room in the Kensington address, so the hanging was a put-up job to throw us off the scent.

'Another fact: Donovan is connected to the address, and his dabs are all over the room where the blood is.

Conclusion: Donovan bumped off Weber.

'Then we come to Mr Seymour Trevelyan, known associate. He has no record – neither does Donovan – but when he goes surety for Donovan, he gives a fictitious address, as does Donovan. Why would you do that? Unless you have something to hide.'

Godley contemplated the recital. 'Will it be enough to get a conviction, sir?'

'Oh yes, Godley – but, just to make sure, I think, at the same time we arrest Donovan, we bring in Seymour Trevelyan. There's a lot he can tell us I'm sure – and now we have the goods on Donovan, I'll wager Trevelyan will be more than happy to turn King's evidence, to save his own neck from the hangman.'

The Man at the Walpole Bay Hotel

'There is one thing, sir.'

Page raised his eyebrows. 'And that is, Godley?'

'Mrs Coates and that message from her housekeeper, sir. Shouldn't we talk to them first? Before we arrest Donovan? The note said they had found the solution.'

Page dismissed the suggestion with a languid flap of his hand. He sniffed and shook his head at the absurdity of the idea. 'I don't think so, lad. It'll be nothing but ladies teatime gossip.'

The afternoon was all but finished when Godley rapped on the door. He had come up with something that had previously been overlooked. 'I found this in the Grayson file, sir.' He put a card down on the desk in front of Page. 'It turned up during the search of Grayson's residence. Nobody thought anything of it at the time – but that was before we knew about the London killing.'

Page picked it up. 'What is it?'

'Invitation, sir – to attend a lecture. Seems Grayson was a member of an ornithological society – based in Holborn – and look at the date; that puts Grayson in London on the same day that German, Ernst Weber, was murdered.'

'Interesting. Well done, Godley.'

'It gets even more interesting, sir. The man delivering the lecture, Mr Bernard Meakin, is a specialist working for the British Museum.'

Page said nothing. He looked at the card, turned it over, tapped it on the table, and thought. 'It isn't proof of a motive, Godley, but it does pull the noose a little tighter.'

The Man at the Walpole Bay Hotel

'There's something else, sir.'

'Tell me.'

'I put in a telephone call to the Library. Benedict Grayson was a member. According to the records, Grayson was there, in the Reading Room, at the same time the librarian reported seeing Weber there. She says she was alerted to Weber by none other than Meakin, who mentioned to her that he thought Weber was acting suspiciously.'

'This gets better all the time. Smart work, Godley.'

Page lifted a fob watch from his top pocket. 'I think it's about time we paid our visit to Mr Donovan, and the doubtful Mr Seymour Trevelyan. Has the constable tailing them called back in recently?'

'He has, sir. They're at the Walpole Bay Hotel. Drinking in the bar.'

'Then the Walpole it is. Alert the desk sergeant, Godley; we need a Black Maria parked round the back. Somewhere discreet, so it can't be seen from the hotel. Right lad, let's get on with it.'

The Man at the Walpole Bay Hotel

Chapter 18

Finale

The Rolls Royce of Ratty Bumstead motored sedately into Margate in convoy with the Prince Henry.

As the town clock came into view, Dorothy blew into the trumpet mouthpiece of the communication tube. A whistling sound in the driver's cab alerted Higgs the chauffeur. 'Yes, madam.'

'Take us to the police station, please, Higgs. After that we shall need to go to the Walpole Bay Hotel.' She turned to Effie and winked. 'I think one of Robson's delicious slammers would be in order – that'll perk us up a bit.'

'Splendid idea. I must say I'm feeling an awful lot better now anyway, but a slammer would rather hit the spot – though I think I should like to go home and change my clothes first; I'm feeling most dreadfully shabby.'

'Just a quick call on Inspector Page, Effie. I want to let him know the lay of the land before he goes off and does something foolish, like arrest Harry again. After that, a quick wash and brush-up.'

*

The desk sergeant at the police station crumpled up his face and drew in a noisy breath. 'I'm sorry, ladies. Strict instructions. Inspector Page is not to be disturbed. Besides, he's gone for his afternoon tea – somewhere in the town. Probably across the way, but I couldn't say exactly.'

Dorothy shot him a look of irritation. 'Well, when will he be back?'

The sergeant returned a blank stare. 'Not today he won't, madam. Try again tomorrow.'

'Ergh!' Dorothy all but screamed through gritted teeth. 'Hopeless! Come along, Effie.'

'Tell you what, ladies,' the sergeant lowered his voice to not much above a whisper; he looked furtively up and down the corridor, then beckoned with a crooked finger, 'you could try the Walpole Bay Hotel – around six.' He tapped a finger against the side of his nose, eyes widened in a knowing look.

Dorothy's demeanour did an about face. 'Thank you,' she smiled, 'in which case Effie, there is time to get dressed up after all. Good afternoon, sergeant.'

Outside the police station the two cars were waiting for them.

The Man at the Walpole Bay Hotel

'Ratty, I'm going to need the services of Higgs,' Dorothy informed him as he sat there at the wheel of the Prince Henry. 'He can take us to our homes and wait while we get changed and cleaned up. Then I shall need him to take us to the Walpole Bay. I would also like you to come along as well – and bring your man with you. I need witnesses. We need to be there no later than six o'clock.' What time is it now?

Ratty consulted his gold hunter. 'Four thirty-five, missus.'

'In that case we have just under one hour and a half. We must get a move on.'

*

'Well I must say that *is* an improvement.' Dorothy looked admiringly as a refreshed Effie came into the drawing room and announced she was ready to go. 'What a lovely outfit,' Dorothy enthused. 'So light and – how should I say – simple and uncluttered.'

'Yes, isn't it a stunner. It's the very latest in new creations from Paris. The oriental look. Paul Poiret. No corset. He says corsets are positively out of style – he's banished them. So he says.'

'Well, you look a knockout.'

'More like I've *been* knocked out, actually.' Effie peered at her image in a large wall mirror. 'Such a nuisance that black eye. Doesn't really go with the dress, would you say?'

'You look divine. Come on; Higgs is waiting and it's almost six.'

The Man at the Walpole Bay Hotel

'Do you suppose Inspector Page will try to arrest Harry?' Effie asked, as they drove along Eastern Esplanade.

'Oh I'm certain. He's such a foolish man. Besides, he clearly doesn't know what we know.'

'Well, he would, Dorothy, if he could just get off his high horse for a moment and listen to you.'

'Indeed. Right, here we are. Slammers first, I think, then we'll see to Inspector Page. Thank you, Higgs.'

As they came into the reception Simpson, the concierge, greeted them. 'Good afternoon, ladies. You are both looking very elegant ... ,' he broke off in mid-sentence. 'Oh dear, what *has* happened?' He cast an embarrassed eye over their faces, trying not to look too shocked.

'Rough-housing, Simpson. Bit of fisticuffs,' Effie grinned, then drew a sharp breath at the pain in her face.

'Set upon by ruffians,' Dorothy joked. 'Gave them a good pasting, though. Not what they were expecting.'

'In that case, well done, ladies. Is there anything I can get for you?'

'Slammers, a couple of Robson's Walpole Bay Slammers, Simpson.'

'Big ones if you would be so good, please,' Effie pitched in. 'We're going through to the lounge. You haven't seen that Inspector Page chappie by any chance?'

'No, not this evening, Mrs Dalrymple.'

The Man at the Walpole Bay Hotel

'Well, if he does appear could you point him to the lounge? Mrs Coates would like to have a word with him.'

Simpson gave a deferential bow of his head. 'Of course, ladies, and I shall get Herbert the waiter to bring you your drinks right away.'

'Awfully nice man, our Simpson,' Effie said, as they went into the lounge. 'Ah look, Harry and Seymour; oh and Lucy too. Shall we join them?'

'I think it's probably the best thing to do. Then we shall have a front row seat when Inspector Page arrives to say his piece ... ooh, speak of the devil, Effie.'

Page, together with Godley and two uniformed constables, strode into the lounge, followed by Simpson and Herber the waiter. 'Your Slammers ladies,' Simpson smiled, 'and also your policeman. Enjoy your cocktails.'

Page stood looking around for a moment, then spotting Donovan made straight for him.

'Were on, Effie. Come along.'

'Oh, drat the man. I've barely had a sip of my drink. Well, I shall just bring it along with me.'

'I think I shall do the same.'

Seeing Page heading towards where he was sitting with Trevelyan and Lucinda, Donovan stood up. The other two followed suit.

'Hello, Inspector.' Donovan broke into an insolent smile, as if he knew what was coming.

Page gave the tiniest rocking nod of his head, several times; his lips pursed. 'Henry Charles Raleigh St George Donovan, I am arresting you

The Man at the Walpole Bay Hotel

for the murder of Benedict Arthur Grayson, and on suspicion of two other murders for which you may be charged later. You are not obliged to say anything, but anything you do say will be taken down in writing and ...'

Before he could finish, a voice from behind him cut him short.

'No, no, no!'

He glanced over his shoulder. 'Oh, no – Mrs Coates! Not now. You are interrupting police business and the proper conduct of the law. I am arresting this man. Now please, go away.'

'I understand what is happening,' Dorothy said firmly, 'but you can't do that.'

Irritation rose in Page's face. Ignoring her presence and keeping a close watch on Donovan, he threw his words over his shoulder at her. 'Might I remind you that obstruction of an officer in the performance of his duty is a serious offence. I should not like to have to ask the constables here to arrest you. Now please desist.'

Dorothy stood her ground. 'You have made a mistake, Inspector,' she said politely.

Page puffed out an exasperated breath. He turned to face them. 'No, Mrs Coates, it is you who are making the mistake by persisting in this manner. Now will you please be good ladies and take yourselves off – both of you.'

'She is right you know,' Effie said cheerfully. 'She's worked it all out. She's very good at these things, you know.'

Page was preparing to issue a stern warning, to order his constables to escort them from the room but he abruptly stopped and, breaking off the conversation, pointed to Effie's black eye. In the same moment he came to notice Dorothy's injuries. 'How did that happen to you?'

'We were attacked,' Dorothy said bluntly.

'Fenians,' threw in Effie. 'That's what this is all about.'

Page huffed his exasperation again. 'What *are* you talking about?'

There was another distraction as Ratty walked in, Higgs and Billy Arden trailing in his wake. 'Sorry I'm a bit late, missus.'

'*Who the hell are this lot*!?' Page waved both hands at the newcomers. 'Would someone mind telling me what is going on?'

'Well we have been trying to for some time, but you just won't listen.' Effie scolded with evident satisfaction. 'Witnesses, they're witnesses.

'Reginald Bumstead,' Dorothy said curtly.

'Ratty to his friends,' Effie butted in.

Ratty grinned, acknowledging Page. 'Evenin.'

'He saw the man who pushed Grayson off the cliff,' Dorothy continued, 'but it wasn't Mr Donovan here.'

Page had taken to sighing. 'No, no that can't be right.'

'Oh it is.' Effie had forgotten the pain in her face and was sporting a broad grin. 'It was mistaken identity, you see. All of it. That cad in the mortuary we thought was Harry – but it wasn't. It was all a mistake, you see.'

The Man at the Walpole Bay Hotel

Page was looking firmly at Effie, 'I think you've had one too many of them,' he said, pointing an accusatory finger at the glass in her hand.

Effie shook her head. 'Positively not, no, this is my first one. Have you tried one of Robson's Slammers – they're awfully good.'

Page shifted his gaze to Dorothy and then the others. 'Can somebody tell me what this lady is talking about?'

'Well, if you will listen, and not keep interrupting, I shall explain,' Dorothy said in a firm voice.

Page gave her a sullen look. 'Very well, go on – but I should caution you, wasting police time is a criminal offence – so it had better be good.'

'Of course it is,' Effie insisted. 'Really, Inspector, sometimes you are the silliest man. Just listen.'

'Mind your language please, madam. Very well, Mrs Coates, proceed.'

Dorothy took a biggish swallow of her drink. 'Ratty, tell the Inspector here what you told me about that night on the clifftop; what you saw when you were out walking old Toby – the night Mr Grayson was killed.'

Ratty eyed Page suspiciously. He was not one to trust a policeman.

'It were about eleven, missus. I were up there wiv Toby, my old lurcher. Ee's a bit past 'is prime so we 'ave ter take it slow. There was this cove, there were two of 'em. They come out'a the Fayreness. Grayson and that fella there.' He

The Man at the Walpole Bay Hotel

pointed to Donovan. 'Not togever like; first Grayson, then 'im. Grayson went over to the cliff edge. Looking through binoculars ee were.'

'Then what happened, Ratty?'

'Me and old Toby went orf as far as the inn at Kingsgate Bay, the Captain Digby. It took us a fair while on account old Toby, ee don't walk so quick.'

'So you keep telling us,' Page said impatiently, 'get to the point, man.'

'Yes, carry on Ratty.'

'Well, missus, old Toby stopped to cock a leg; can't 'old his bladder no more. While we was waiting I see this fella 'ere.' He pointed again to Donovan. 'Ee gave a wave to Grayson and walked orf – like ee were away ter Palm Bay. Then this other cove, ee appeared. I think ee come up from the beach. Mind you, I only saw 'im from 'is back. Ee'd walked up behind Grayson. I looked down to attend on old Toby and when I looked up again, well, Grayson were gorn. This other cove ee were walking orf double quick; went down the path ter the beach.'

Page narrowed his eyes. 'Did you see this man's face?'

'Nah, like I said, just the back of 'im.'

'One thing more, Ratty,' Dorothy said. 'Harry, will you just turn your back to us.'

Donovan turned to face the wall. 'Would you say that Harry there looks a bit like Mr Grayson – when viewed from behind? Grayson was wearing something like a Panama that night, I believe. Harry, you wear a Panama don't you?'

'I do.' Donovan picked up his hat from where it rested on a chair and waved it.

'Could you oblige us and put it on. Right-ho, Ratty. What do you think?'

Ratty grinned. 'Yeah, you're sharp as a razor, missus. Now you see 'im like that, ee's a dead ringer for that Grayson from behind.'

'Thank you, Ratty. So you see, Inspector, mistaken identity.'

'All right, but in that case, Mrs Coates, who did kill Grayson – and more to the point, why?'

'The same killer who murdered the second man, Inspector, that salesman chappie from Canterbury, Sanderson – and he did it with the same motive.'

'So – *who was he*!?'

'I'll come to that in a minute. Let's look at the why of it. Why would anyone want to kill a rather unremarkable travelling salesman? A jealous lover perhaps? According to Sanderson's wife he had a bit of a roving eye. Perhaps even a vengeful husband whose wife Sanderson had compromised, or even an angry father with a despoiled daughter. All possible.'

Page turned up his nose disparagingly. 'I don't think so, Mrs Coates; the Canterbury police could find no evidence to support that.'

'No, and I'm not surprised, because Sanderson was killed for none of those reasons. He was killed because our murderer thought he was somebody else. Another case of mistaken identity. He was the wrong man; an innocent victim.'

The Man at the Walpole Bay Hotel

'So, hold on a minute. You say this man killed Grayson – for a reason you have not yet disclosed?'

'Correct, Inspector.'

'So why would he want to go on and kill Sanderson? That doesn't add up.'

'Well, it does if you understand that both these murders were connected by one thing – they were both mistaken identities. When our killer was told he had done in the wrong man, he went out in search of the right man. Unfortunately, he killed the wrong man a second time.'

'Are you saying the murderer did not personally know his victims, Mrs Coates?'

'Precisely, Inspector. Because this was what our American cousins call a contract killing. The murderer was a hit man. He did not know his victims personally. He was simply paid to do the job. He killed the wrong man – twice, the more regrettably. They were killed because, rather unluckily, they both looked like the intended victim when viewed from behind.'

She broke off and turned to Effie. 'It was your story about Max in the Tiergarten that made the penny drop for me.'

Page looked unconvinced. 'So you say, Mrs Coates, so you say. But this is all conjecture if I may say so. I mean, if your guesswork, and that's what it is, is correct – and I don't see the evidence at the moment. That still leaves us with the unanswered question: who *was* the intended victim?'

The Man at the Walpole Bay Hotel

Dorothy looked at Page and smiled. 'Why, Inspector, I thought even *you* might have guessed that by now – it was him.' Dorothy pointed directly at Donovan. 'Wasn't it, Harry?' Donovan smiled but said nothing.

Page's face filled with scepticism. 'Oh really, Mrs Coates. I mean to say, what makes you think that?'

'Two things, Inspector. As Ratty said, viewed from behind, Harry was a dead ringer for Grayson, and you may recall that even with his face burned, Sanderson had an uncanny likeness to Harry.'

Page shrugged one shoulder and tightened his mouth. He looked moodily at Dorothy. He didn't much care to be told how to do his job; even less when the person telling him was a woman. He graced her with a patronising smile, slowly shaking his head in rebuttal. 'No, no, that doesn't make sense. Why would someone want to kill this man?'

Dorothy did not reply; instead she looked over at Donovan and nodded. 'We'll come to that too, Inspector.'

Donovan still said nothing; just a hint of humour in his look. It was clear he was enjoying the act being played out in front of him.

Page lost patience. 'Well,' he said wearily, 'let's hear it, Mrs Coates.'

'We have to start with the death of Ernst Weber.'

'*What's he got to do with it!?*' Page looked like he would explode.

The Man at the Walpole Bay Hotel

'Well – everything really. As you know, Weber was a secretary at the German Embassy in Washington. When Britain declared war on Germany, a group from Philadelphia, Clan na Gael, approached the embassy to arrange a secret meeting. The Clan are Irish Americans; supporters of the free Eire movement, Fenians. They wanted help for the cause from Germany. Not money, – just arms, guns and ammunition for a revolt against us, the British in Ireland. An agreement was struck and things would have proceeded smoothly – but for one thing. The secretary who took the minutes for the meeting and who drew up the agreement, Ernst Weber, decided there was an opportunity. He took the documents and came with them to London.'

'For what purpose?'

'For money, of course, Inspector. He recognised there could be value in the documents to the British and aimed to profit from them. Simply a cash transaction.

'In London he contacted someone he knew from his work in Washington. Someone with good connections, someone to act as a commission agent between him and a party interested in paying money to acquire the papers: a go-between.

'But something went wrong. The word got out. Two Fenians were sent from Dublin to dispose of Weber and get back the documents. There was a third man as well – what you might call a fixer – who had been sent over from America to make sure the guns were landed safely and then reached their destination. He also happened to be a hit man

– though, that was not what he was originally sent over for.

'Weber was tracked to the British Museum Library, where he had arranged a rendezvous with the go-between. When he realised the Fenians were onto him, he hid the documents inside a book – an illustrated work on oystercatchers – then bolted. He thought he had given them the slip. What he did not know was that the third man, the fixer now turned hired killer, had picked up his trail and was following a few yards behind him. Now Weber made a fatal error. He went to an address in Kensington, to the house of his contact, the go-between. The cleaning lady opened the door. She had seen Weber at the house before, so let him in. Sometime after she left, the killer managed to gain entry to the house and murder Weber. When the go-between turned up, Weber was already dead.'

'All right,' Page said impatiently, 'very entertaining, I'm sure, but this is all conjecture – and *who* is this mystery American? I need facts, Mrs Coates, not guesses. I have to have corroboration, a suspect I can arrest. Now, perhaps you'll be so good as to let me get on with my job.'

'Oh dear,' Effie tutted. 'You are a most vexatious man. She is coming to that – are you not, Dorothy?'

'Indeed, Effie. The man who killed Ernst Weber was the same man who pushed Grayson off the clifftop and killed Sanderson, neither of whom were connected in any way other than on each occasion they were mistaken for Henry Donovan.'

The Man at the Walpole Bay Hotel

'He wasn't a very bright man, you see.' Effie smiled sweetly at Page and took a sip of her cocktail.

Page shot a glance at Donovan. 'Wait a minute. You claim to be a birdwatcher, and so is Miss Lucinda Coates, and she works for the British Museum. Now I see it. You got that book on oystercatchers didn't you? Those Fenians thought you had the documents. That's why they came after you?' Donovan looked at Trevelyan, who smiled benignly. Lucinda glanced from one to the other, a puzzled expression on her face.

'Close, Inspector,' Dorothy said, 'though not quite right. You see, Harry is not at all what he claims to be; nor is his friend Mr Trevelyan. Shall I tell them, Seymour, or will you?'

Trevelyan offered an exaggerated bow. 'Please, be my guest Dorothy. I thought perhaps you had not remembered me.'

Dorothy raised an eyebrow. 'Calcutta, Seymour. Who could forget a Viceroy's party?'

'What *is* this all about?' Page said grumpily.

'The reason they wanted Harry dead, of course. You see, Inspector, Harry Donovan *was* the go-between, and Harry is an agent of the government secret service, MI5. Seymour is his boss. Simple really. They've been watching those Fenians for a while now, but then things went wrong, not the least of the reasons being that my niece Lucy loaned me the book on oystercatchers. I found the documents tucked inside the pages, so I gave them to my friend, Mrs Dalrymple.'

'I'm confused,' Page said. 'Is that important?'

'Oh, yes,' Effie piped up. 'I'm fluent in German. I made a translation.'

'Which,' Dorothy said, 'is what aroused our interest in the case.'

'They chased after them Fenians,' Ratty chimed in. 'They shouldn't of done that. I warned 'em not to – but they didn't take no notice, did they. That's who duffed 'em up. Gave 'em them shiners.'

'And I must say, Dorothy … ,' Trevelyan wagged an admonishing finger, '… you rather blew our cover with the Irishmen.'

'Sorry, Seymour.'

Page's head swivelled back and forth, his eyes flicking from one speaker to another. 'Wait a minute, wait a minute. What is all this? And why wasn't I told about the involvement of MI5? This is highly irregular.'

Trevelyan raised a hand. 'Apologies, Inspector. Secrecy was paramount, you see. We knew there was a danger that Mrs Coates and her friend might get into difficulties, but we had to keep our heads down.'

'Yes, sorry,' Donovan said shyly. 'I kept my fingers crossed they wouldn't do for you.'

'They very nearly did, Harry. It was only thanks to Effie that we're not both dead. Luckily she had her husband's gun. She had to shoot one of them.'

'*Hold on a minute!*' Page looked at Effie, horrified. 'Do I understand you shot someone, madam?'

'I only wounded him, Inspector, not dead,' she thought for a moment, 'at least, not when we last saw him. He was bleeding rather lot, though.'

The Man at the Walpole Bay Hotel

'Do you have a licence for this gun you're shooting people with?'

'No, afraid not,' Effie said sheepishly. 'It was my husband's. He died. I still have it. A sort of keepsake.'

Page looked as if he was preparing for stern words but Dorothy cut him off short.

'No matter that, Inspector. The man you want for the murders is one Jackson Molloy of Boston, Massachusetts. He was with the Fenians and a truck full of guns. They were heading for Southampton. Molloy had a passage booked from there to New York. The Fenians were taking the guns to Bristol after that. They have a private yacht waiting for them: the *Regina Maris*; ready to sail for Dublin.'

'I don't think he'll get very far,' Effie said. 'I shot him in the foot so he can't move very quickly.'

Page looked like he might choke. '*Mrs Dalrymple*! You *can't* go about the country *shooting* people. It's against the law.'

'Well, they were jolly beastly – and it was self-defence.'

'Never mind all that,' Dorothy interrupted. 'We alerted the constables at Ashford. Molloy and the Fenians should all be in custody by now.'

Page shuffled uncomfortably. He cast an eye across the assembled faces, not sure what to say. 'Very well,' he eventually said. 'Godley, get in touch with Ashford. See if they've nabbed this Molloy character and the other two. Then get the constables back to the station. We shan't be needing them – or the Black Maria.'

He turned back to Dorothy. There is one thing you may be able to clear up. We found out that Grayson was a member of the British Museum Library. He was there when Weber was. What was he doing there?'

Dorothy shrugged and raised her eyebrows. 'Borrowing a book? I have no idea, Inspector. Probably a coincidence. Not everything that turns up is connected – even when it looks that way.'

*

'Pretty good show, Dorothy,' Seymour Trevelyan raised a respectful finger in a sort of salute. 'You should think about becoming a private eye. You seem to have a talent.'

'Well, thank you, Seymour. I feel flattered. I might even take up that idea. But there is one thing I don't fully understand.'

'Which is?'

'The German papers, the minutes and that memorandum. Why did you want them so badly that you were prepared to break into my friend Effie's house? I take it that was you?'

'Not me personally, of course – I merely arranged for it to happen.'

'I still don't understand. Surely if you knew the agreement to supply the guns had been made, those papers wouldn't matter – would they?' Trevelyan screwed up his face and considered the question.

The Man at the Walpole Bay Hotel

'Go on, Seymour,' Donovan grinned. 'It's not a state secret.'

'True, but could be embarrassing, dear boy. I mean, if the story got out, that is.'

Dorothy pinned him with a hard stare. 'And – are you going to tell?'

'Right ho, but strictly *entre nous,* old thing. No names, no pack drill. Wouldn't want it getting out generally. A certain politician – high up in the government, shall we say. He wanted the papers to reinforce the government's decision for the declaration of war. A sort of back-up vindication.'

'Was that necessary?' Lucinda said, surprised. 'The Germans were the aggressors after all.'

Trevelyan raised a hand. 'Ha, Lucy, my dear girl. If only politics were that straightforward. Not everybody sees it that way, you know. Anyway, my masters thought the papers worth paying for. They paid up – *ergo* I was under pressure to come up with the goods, as they like to say.'

Dorothy looked knowingly at Trevelyan. 'And I suppose you would like our copy?'

'A copy would be better than nothing, dear thing.'

'Oh no, it isn't a copy,' Effie piped up. 'I have the originals. The copy was what those ruffian Fenians stole from Dorothy's house. The very idea of breaking in. It makes one shudder.'

'There you go, Seymour, you are now in my debt for two favours.'

'Two, Dorothy? How so?'

'A discreetly patched up face. Do you not remember?'

The Man at the Walpole Bay Hotel

'Ah yes, George. Eternally grateful. Sorry to hear he died so young.'

'What was that cut on your face all about anyway, Seymour? Do tell.'

Trevelyan shook his head and looked rueful. 'Fraid can't say, old thing. State secret and all that humbug, don'tcha know.'

'Ah, here's Simpson,' Effie announced. 'I'd say that calls for a glass of something. Perhaps Slammers all round?'

Simpson put a silver bucket on the table.

'Oh boy, champagne,' Dorothy enthused, 'Ayala 1904. I say, that's rather swish. On you is it, Seymour?'

'Not me, dear girl. I'm not that flush, you know.'

'You, Harry?'

Simpson inclined his head towards the bucket. 'Compliments of Mr Bumstead, ladies.' He opened the bottle with no more than the slightest whisper of fizz as he eased out the cork. Glasses were charged.

'Well, here's to Ratty,' Effie proposed, raising her glass. 'Is he still here, Simpson?'

'No, Mrs Dalrymple, he left. He said to convey his apologies but he had business matters to attend. Something to do with the recovery of some lost monies, I understand.'

'Well, bless him anyway,' Dorothy smiled, taking a sip. 'I say, it's almost time for dinner. Shall we stay here? Seymour, Harry, will you join us?'

The Man at the Walpole Bay Hotel

'Regrets, old thing,' Seymour said. 'Have to get back to London. Can't speak for Harry.'

'Harry's taking me to the Winter Gardens.' Lucinda slipped her arm through his. 'Aren't you, Harry?'

'Well – err – yes, of course.'

'Good, that's settled, and this time you won't have to fence about with talk of oystercatchers.'

'It was whimbrels, actually.'

'No, Harry, not whimbrels – curlews. Similar bird but wrong time of the year for whimbrels.' She gave his arm a squeeze. 'Your knowledge of wading birds really is horribly lamentable.'

'Right Effie, it'll be just the two of us for dinner then,' Dorothy said after the others had left them.

She took a compact from her handbag, opened it and stared critically into the tiny mirror. 'It's going to take a few days to be rid of these shiners. I saw a woman looking at me earlier when we arrived. I suspect she thought I'd been knocked about by a disgruntled husband.'

'Yes, I got the same sort of look from the girl on reception. At least Simpson showed some decorum. Not more than the blink of an eye.'

'The essence of discretion, dear Simpson. Ah, here he is now.'

Simpson gestured towards the bucket and the empty champagne bottle. 'May I clear this away, ladies?'

'Of course,' Dorothy said, 'and can we have our usual table for dinner?'

'Certainly, Mrs Coates. I shall arrange it right away. Is there anything else?'

'I think there's just time for two more of Robson's delicious Walpole Bay Slammers – how say you, Effie?

'Oooh *ra-ther.*'

Printed in Great Britain
by Amazon